John Webster's The White Devil: A Retelling

David Bruce

Published by David Bruce, 2022.

This is a work of fiction. Similarities to real people, places, or events are entirely coincidental.

JOHN WEBSTER'S THE WHITE DEVIL: A RETELLING

First edition. July 19, 2022.

Copyright © 2022 David Bruce.

ISBN: 979-8201009663

Written by David Bruce.

Table of Contents

Dedication

Dedicated to My Uncle Reuben Saturday

When he was a young man, my mother's brother Reuben wanted to escape from poverty and lard sandwiches, so he tried to run away from it. He stole a car so he could drive up north where he hoped to find opportunity, but he got caught and ended up on a Georgia chain gang for several months. In a chain gang, prisoners are shackled every few feet by the ankles to a long length of chain to keep them from escaping. They work in the hot sun while shackled to the chain, and when they sleep, they are shackled to the bed. No freedom, hard work, hot sun, no pay, bad food, and some mean guards.

When my uncle got released from the chain gang, he hitchhiked up north. He did what a lot of people trying to escape from poverty do: He drifted. He drifted from town to town, seeking opportunity and not finding it. He worked when he could, but the jobs were temporary and low pay. My uncle slept rough often, and he was hungry often. Once, when he was completely broke and completely hungry, he saw a restaurant with a buffet and went inside and asked to speak to the manager. He said, "I am very hungry, I don't have any money, and I would appreciate it very much if you would give me any food that the restaurant is going to throw away. I will be happy to wait by the rear entrance until you are ready to throw away food."

The manager told him to sit down at a table, and then the manager went to the buffet, loaded a big plate high with food, and gave it to him free of charge.

One way out of poverty is to get a good job, and my uncle got out of poverty by getting a job working with sheet metal.

My uncle's work ethic helped him. His employer sent him to California to do some special sheet-metal work, and the people in California wanted to keep him there. They explained that their California employees liked to come to work late, leave early, and take many days off. It was difficult to get someone who would show up and do the work they were supposed to do and were paid to do.

My uncle was also good with money. He got married, bought a house, and raised six children. Each time he made a mortgage payment, he paid extra money so he could pay off the mortgage faster.

If there was a sale on food, he bought lots of it. For example, if there was a sale on peanut butter, two jars for the price of one, he would buy twelve jars and sometimes go back the next day and buy six more jars.

If you went in his pantry — a closet set aside to store food — you saw that it was packed with food. If you went in his kitchen, you saw that he had taken off the doors of the high cabinets in which he stored food so that he could see the food. If you went in his bedroom, you saw that he had all the regular bedroom furniture, but he also had lots of shelves he had installed. The shelves were loaded with things that he had bought on sale that he knew his family could use: food (of course), light bulbs, toothpaste, toilet paper, etc. His bedroom looked like a warehouse.

Once he made a bad purchase: he bought a case of baked beans. Beans are beans, but the sauce they came in can taste good or bad, and the sauce these beans came in tasted bad. His kids told him, "Dad, throw those beans away! They're awful!"

But when you grow up poor, you don't throw beans away. For a long time, whenever my uncle and his family ate baked beans, they ate a mixture of one can of good baked beans and one can of bad baked beans.

My uncle's kids never had to eat lard sandwiches.

***

The doing of good deeds is important. As a free person, you can choose to live your life as a good person or as a bad person. To be a good person, do good deeds. To be a bad person, do bad deeds. If you do good deeds, you will become good. If you do bad deeds, you will become bad. To become the person you want to be, act as if you already are that kind of person. Each of us chooses what kind of person we will become. To become a good person, do the things a good person does. To become a bad person, do the things a bad person does. The opportunity to take action to become the kind of person you want to be is yours.

Cover Photograph for John Webster's *The White Devil*: A Retelling : https://pixabay.com/photos/man-mask-blue-eyes-hand-mystery-1461448/

Educate Yourself
Read Like A Wolf Eats
Be Excellent to Each Other
Books Then, Books Now, Books Forever

***

In this retelling, as in all my retellings, I have tried to make the work of literature accessible to modern readers who may lack some of the knowledge about mythology, religion, and history that the literary work's contemporary audience had.

Do you know a language other than English? If you do, I give you permission to translate this book, copyright your translation, publish or self-publish it, and keep all the royalties for yourself. (Do give me credit, of course, for the original retelling.)

I would like to see my retellings of classic literature used in schools, so I give permission to the country of Finland (and all other countries) to give copies of this book to all students forever. I also give permission to the state of Texas (and all other states) to give copies of this book to all students forever. I also give permission to all teachers to give copies of this book to all students forever.

Teachers need not actually teach my retellings. Teachers are welcome to give students copies of my eBooks as background material. For example, if they are teaching Homer's *Iliad* and *Odyssey*, teachers are welcome to give students copies of my *Virgil's* Aeneid: *A Retelling in Prose* and tell students, "Here's another ancient epic you may want to read in your spare time."

CAST OF CHARACTERS

Male Characters

MONTICELSO, a Cardinal; afterwards Pope PAUL the Fourth. CAMILLO is his nephew.

FRANCISCO DE MEDICI, Duke of Florence; in the 5th Act disguised as a Moor, under the name of MULINASSAR. Brother to ISABELLA.

BRACHIANO, otherwise PAULO GIORDANO URSINI, Duke of Brachiano, Husband to ISABELLA, and in love with VITTORIA.

GIOVANNI, his Son by ISABELLA.

LODOVICO, an Italian Count, but decayed. In the play, he is also called Lodowick. This retelling uses "Lodovico" consistently.

ANTONELLI, GASPARO, his Friends, and Dependents of the Duke of Florence.

CAMILLO, Husband to VITTORIA. Cardinal MONTICELSO is his uncle.

HORTENSIO, one of BRACHIANO's Officers.

MARCELLO, an Attendant of the Duke of Florence, and Brother to FLAMINEO and VITTORIA.

FLAMINEO, Brother to MARCELLO and VITTORIA; Secretary to BRACHIANO.

CARLO and PEDRO: Conspirators with the Duke of Florence.

JACQUES, a young Moor, Servant to GIOVANNI.

CHRISTOPHERO, an assassin.

Female Characters

ISABELLA, Sister to FRANCISCO DE MEDICI, and Wife to BRACHIANO.

VITTORIA COROMBONA, a Venetian Lady; first married to CAMILLO, afterwards to BRACHIANO.

CORNELIA, Mother to VITTORIA, FLAMINEO, and MARCELLO.

ZANCHE, a Moor, Servant to VITTORIA.

Minor Characters

Six Ambassadors, Courtiers, Lawyers, Officers, Physicians, Conjurer, Chancellor, Registrar, Armorer, Attendants.

THE SCENE — ITALY

Notes:

Brachiano is the Duke of Brachiano.

A proverb stated, "The white devil is worse than the black."

A white devil is an evil person who pretends to be a good person.

Possibly, a white devil is a good person whom everyone believes to be evil.

In Elizabethan culture, a man of higher rank would use words such as "thee," "thy," "thine," and "thou" to refer to a servant. However, two close friends or a husband and wife could properly use "thee," "thy," "thine," and "thou" to refer to each other.

The word "sirrah" is a term usually used to address a man of lower social rank than the speaker. This was socially acceptable, but sometimes the speaker would use the word as an insult when speaking to a man whom he did not usually call "sirrah." Close friends, whether male or female, could also call each other "sirrah." Fathers could call their sons "sirrah."

This society believed that the mixture of four humors in the body determined one's temperament. One humor could be predominant. The four humors are blood, yellow bile, black bile, and phlegm. If blood is predominant, then the person is sanguine (optimistic). If yellow bile is predominant, then the person is choleric (bad-tempered). If black bile is predominant, then the person is melancholic (sad). If phlegm is predominant, then the person is phlegmatic (calm). If a person were ill, the illness was caused by an imbalance of humors. The humors could be put back into balance through such things as bloodletting or purging.

CHAPTER 1

— 1.1 —

In Rome, Italy, Antonelli and Gasparo entered a room in which was Count Lodovico, who was waiting to find out how he would be punished for his crimes. Antonelli and Gasparo were Count Lodovico's friends.

Lodovico asked, "Am I banished?"

Antonelli nodded and replied, "It grieved me much to hear the sentence."

"Ha, ha," Lodovico said. "Oh, Democritus, thy two gods who govern the whole world are courtly reward and punishment."

Democritus was an ancient Greek philosopher.

Lodovico continued, "Lady Fortune is a complete whore. If she gives anything, she deals it out in small portions, so that she may take it all away at one swoop."

A "swoop" is 1) a stroke, and/or 2) a commercial deal.

He continued, "This is what it is to have great, important enemies! May God requite them. Your wolf no longer seems to be a wolf except when she's hungry."

A hungry, needy man must show a wolfish nature — for example, when he must rob someone in order to get food. But wealthy people can hide their wolfish nature until they wish to display it.

Gasparo said, "You call those enemies men of princely rank."

"Oh, I pray for them," Lodovico said. "The violent thunder is adored by those who are smashed into pieces by it."

"Come, my lord," Antonelli said. "You are justly sentenced. Look just a little back into your former life. You have in the last three years ruined the noblest earldom."

Counts and earls are the same in rank. A Continental count is socially equivalent to an English earl.

Gasparo said, "Your followers have swallowed you, like mummia, and being sick with such unnatural and horrid medicine, they vomit you up in the gutter."

Mummia was a medicine that was made from human mummies, or from dried human corpses.

Antonelli said, "You have staggered through all the damnable degrees of drinking.

"One wealthy citizen, who is the lord of two fair manors, called you master, only so he could get caviar from you."

Gasparo said, "Those noblemen who were invited to your prodigal feasts, in which the phoenix, only one of which exists at a time, scarcely could escape being swallowed by your throats, laugh at your misery, fore-judging you to be a worthless falling star made up of noxious mists drawn from the earth and certain to be soon dissipated in the air."

Antonelli said, "They make jests about you, and they say you must have been begotten in an earthquake because you have ruined such fair lordships."

"Very good," Lodovico said. "This well goes with two buckets: I must attend to the pouring out of each."

Lodovico was the well, and Antonelli and Gasparo were the buckets that, as one was being filled, the other was being emptied. They were taking turns pouring out bad news and criticism to Lodovico.

"Worse than these," Gasparo said, "you have brought about certain murders here in Rome, murders that are bloody and full of horror."

Lodovico said, "Ah, they were flea bites.

"Why then didn't the authorities take my head?"

Lodovico could have been beheaded to pay for his crimes.

"Oh, my lord!" Gasparo said. "The law sometimes mediates — avoids extremes and settles cases by mediation. The law thinks that it is good to not always steep violent sins in blood. This gentle penance of banishment may both end your crimes, and by force of the example better these bad times."

Lodovico said, "So be it, but I wonder then how it is some great men escape this banishment. There's Paulo Giordano Ursini — the Duke of Brachiano — who now lives in Rome, and by secret panderism seeks to prostitute the honor of Vittoria Corombona — she who might have gotten my pardon by giving one kiss to the duke."

Paulo Giordano Ursini, the Duke of Brachiano, had fallen in love with Vittoria Corombona although they were married to other people.

If Vittoria were to kiss the Duke of Brachiano and request that he go to the pope and ask that Lodovico be pardoned, the Duke of Brachiano would do what he was requested to do.

Antonelli said, "Have a full man within you: Be resolute and fortified. We see that trees bear no such pleasant fruit there where they grew first, as where they are transplanted. Perfumes, the more they are rubbed, the more they render their pleasing scents, and so affliction presses out virtue fully, whether true, or impure."

Proverbs seldom provide comfort to the sufferer, although they may console the comforter.

Lodovico said, "Stop with your false comforts. I'll make Italian cut-works in my enemies' guts if I ever return."

"Cut-works" are openwork embroidery. Lodovico was threatening to put holes — such as those made by swords and daggers — in the bodies of his enemies.

"Oh, sir," Gasparo said.

"I am patient," Lodovico said. "I have seen some who are ready to be executed give pleasant looks and money to and have grown familiar with the knave hangman. So do I. I thank them, and I would account them nobly merciful, if they would dispatch me quickly."

Hangmen are executioners; they can dispatch — kill — quickly, or slowly. It is a good idea to be on good terms with your executioner.

Lodovico was intending to give money to his own kind of executioners — two people who would execute his orders to try to get his banishment repealed.

"Fare you well," Antonelli said. "We shall find the right time, I don't doubt, to repeal your banishment."

A sennet sounded to announce that some important people were arriving.

Lodovico said, "I am forever bound to you."

He gave them some money and said, "This is the world's alms; please make use of it."

The money was for their future help in getting his sentence of banishment lifted. Lodovico, however, was also referring to a proverb as his alms — the proverb stated what the world had taught him and it was something that others could benefit from knowing.

He stated the proverb:

"Great men sell sheep, thus to be cut in pieces,

"When first they have shorn them bare, and sold their fleeces."

Brachiano, Camillo, Flamineo, and Vittoria Corombona talked together in a room in Camillo's house in Rome. Camillo was Vittoria's husband. Flamineo was Vittoria's brother and Brachiano's secretary. Brachiano, who was a duke, loved Vittoria. Some gentlemen were holding torches to provide extra light.

Brachiano said to Camillo and Vittoria, "I wish you the best of rest. May you sleep well."

Vittoria replied, "To my lord the duke, we give the best of welcome."

She ordered the gentlemen attendants, "More lights. Serve the duke."

Camillo and Vittoria exited.

Brachiano said, "Flamineo."

"My lord," he answered.

"I am quite lost, Flamineo," Brachiano said.

Flamineo replied, "Pursue your noble wishes. I am as prompt as lightning at serving you."

He then whispered to Brachiano, "Oh, my lord! The fair Vittoria, my happy sister, shall receive you soon."

He then said to the torch-bearers, "Gentlemen, let the caroche go on."

A caroche is a stately coach.

Flamineo added, "And it is his pleasure that you put out all your torches and depart."

They put out all their torches and departed.

"Are we so happy?" Brachiano asked.

He hoped that Vittoria, Flamineo's sister, would soon visit him. That would make him happy.

"Can it be otherwise?" Flamineo asked. "Didn't you see tonight, my honored lord, that whichever way you went, Vittoria threw her eyes?

"I have dealt already with her chambermaid, Zanche the Moor, and she is wondrously proud to be the agent for so high a spirit."

Brachiano said, "We are happy above thought, because above merit."

"Above merit!" Flamineo said.

He looked, saw that the gentlemen torch-bearers had left, and said, "We may now talk freely. Above merit! What is it you doubt and fear? Her coyness!

That's only the superficies of lust — false persona regarding lust — that most women have."

Even lustful women are concerned about their reputations and pretend to be coy and shy when they are not.

Flamineo continued, "Yet why should ladies blush to hear that named, which they do not fear to handle?"

The verb "handle" can mean 1) touch, and/or 2) talk about.

He continued, "Oh, they are politic and cunning; they know that our desire is increased by the difficulty of enjoying, whereas satiety is a blunt, weary, and drowsy passion. If the buttery-hatch at court stood continually open, there would not be a passionate crowding, nor a hot suit after the beverage."

The buttery was a storeroom for alcoholic beverages. Butteries had doors made of half-doors. The top half was open when beverages were being served from the buttery.

Brachiano said, "Oh, but her jealous husband —"

Flamineo interrupted, "Hang him.

"A gilder who has his brains perished with quicksilver is not more cold in the liver."

Gilders used quicksilver (mercury) and gold while gilding items. The quicksilver, which is poisonous, was burned off, and gilders who inhaled too much of the poisonous vapor could suffer from tremors and insanity. According to this society, the liver was the seat of passion. Flamineo was saying that Camillo, Vittoria's husband, lacked sexual passion.

Flamineo continued, "The great barriers molted not more feathers than he has shed hairs, by the confession of his doctor."

During martial tournaments, two men could fight with short swords or pikes with a waist-high barrier between them, thus reducing the chance of a serious accident. During the fights, the feathered plumes of their helmets could be shaken or cut off. Older, bald men do not have the sexual vigor of young men. Camillo was not old, but Flamineo was saying that he had the same lack of sexual vigor that many old men have. Baldness was also a side effect of treatments for syphilis, a disease that can interfere with having further sex.

Flamineo continued, "An Irish gamester who will play himself naked, and then wage all downward, putting all at hazard, is not more venturous."

Wild Irishmen were said to gamble away all their clothing and then, having nothing else to wager, gamble away their testicles. Flamineo was saying that because Camillo's testicles were of no use to him, he was as willing as the wild Irishmen to gamble them away.

Flamineo continued, "He is so unable to please a woman, that, like a Dutch doublet, all his back is shrunk into his breaches."

The Dutch wore close-fitting doublets (jackets) and wide, baggy trousers. A shrunken back is a weak back and a man's weak back is a sign that he is unable to have sex.

Flamineo continued, "Shroud you within this closet, my good lord."

He wanted Brachiano to hide where he could see (and sometimes hear) other people but not be seen by them.

Flamineo continued, "Some trick now must be thought on to divide my brother-in-law from his fair bedfellow."

Vittoria had agreed to meet Brachiano that night, but her husband had to be gotten out of the way first.

Brachiano said, "Oh, should she fail to come —"

Flamineo said, "I must not have your lordship thus unwisely amorous. I myself have loved a lady and pursued her with a great deal of under-age protestation — youthful, immature declarations of love. I did this at a time when some three or four gallants who have enjoyed this lady would with all their hearts have been glad to have been rid of her."

Flamineo believed that Brachiano would be successful with Vittoria, Flamineo's sister, and so Brachiano's fear that Vittoria would not show up was unwisely amorous.

It was also, of course, unwisely amorous because Brachiano and Vittoria were both married, but not to each other.

Flamineo himself knew what it was like to be unwisely amorous — he had pursued a lady whom others had already slept with and wanted to get rid of.

Flamineo continued, "It is just like a summer bird-cage in a garden: The birds that are outside despair to get in, and the birds that are within despair and are sick out of fear they shall never get out."

Birds and people want what they don't have.

Flamineo continued, "Away, away, my lord. Hide yourself."

Brachiano hid himself as Camillo entered the room.

Flamineo whispered to the hidden Brachiano, "See, here he comes. Some men would judge this fellow to be a politician by his apparel, but call his intelligence into question, and you shall find it is merely an ass in a footcloth."

A footcloth was a fancy cloth that hung from a horse ridden by a high-ranking man. Flamineo was saying that Camillo looked like an intelligent man because of his clothing, but a quick examination of his "intelligence" would reveal that he was really an ass.

"How are you now, brother-in-law?" Flamineo asked Camillo. "What, travelling to bed with your kind wife?"

Flamineo thought, *The word "traveling" sounds much like "travailing." For Camillo, having sex with his wife is a travail — it is painful and takes an effort.*

"I assure you, brother-in-law, no," Camillo said. "My voyage lies more northerly, in a far colder clime. I do not well remember, I say, when I last lay with her."

Flamineo said, "It is strange you should lose your count."

Flamineo thought, *He has lost his cunt.*

Camillo said, "We never lay together but before morning there grew a flaw between us."

In other words: Each time they lay together, an argument would occur between them before the morning.

A flaw is a squall, which could part two ships that were close together. Figuratively, it is an argument. A flaw is also a crack. Figuratively, it is a vulva.

Flamineo said, "It had been your part to have made up that flaw."

Camillo could have acted in such a way to make up their differences and stop the argument.

One way to "make up" or fix a flaw, aka a crack, is to fill it.

Flamineo was saying that one way for Camillo to fix the quarrel between him and his wife was to fill her vagina.

Camillo replied, "True, but she loathes that I should be seen in it."

"Why, sir, what's the matter?" Flamineo asked.

Camillo said, "The duke — your master — visits me, and I thank him."

Brachiano was the Duke of Brachiano.

Camillo continued, "And I perceive how, like an earnest bowler, he very passionately leans the way he would have his bowl run."

The game of bowls was played with balls. Camillo knew that Brachiano was interested in Vittoria.

Flamineo said, "I hope you do not think —"

Camillo interrupted, "That noblemen bowl booty?"

"Bowl booty" occurred when two players conspired to defeat a third player. Right now, Brachiano and Flamineo were conspiring to make Camillo a cuckold — a man with an unfaithful wife.

Camillo continued, "In faith, his cheek has a most excellent bias: it would like to jump with my mistress."

A cheek is the rounded surface of a bowl (ball). A bias is the weighted side of a ball used in the game of bowls: The balls were not perfectly round but were weighted on one side so that they would roll erratically: They were lopsided. A mistress is the small white ball at which the larger bowls (balls) were aimed. To jump with the mistress is to run up against and touch the mistress.

Of course, these terms had sexual meanings. For example, to jump a mistress meant to have sex with her.

Flamineo asked, "Will you be an ass, despite your Aristotle?"

Aristotle was an ancient Greek philosopher. "Despite your Aristotle" meant "despite your learning."

Flamineo continued, "Or a cuckold, contrary to your ephemerides, which show you under what a smiling planet you were first swaddled?"

Ephemerides are tables of astrological data in almanacs.

A smiling planet was a fortuitous sign. According to astrology, being born under a smiling planet meant that one would have a fortuitous life and so one ought not to worry about bad things that won't happen.

Camillo said, "Bah, sir. Don't tell me about planets and don't tell me about ephemerides. A man may be made a cuckold in the daytime, when the stars' eyes are out."

Flamineo said, "Sir, goodbye. I commit you to your pitiful pillow stuffed with horn-shavings."

Cuckolds were said to have horns growing out of their forehead. Flamineo was saying that Camillo had shaved off his cuckold's horns.

Camillo said, "Brother-in-law!"

Flamineo said, "May God refuse to allow me into Paradise if I were to advise you now that your only course would be to lock up your wife —"

Camillo said, "That would be very good advice."

Flamineo continued, "— keep her from the sight of revels —"

Camillo said, "Excellent advice."

Flamineo continued, "— let her not go to church, unless, like a hound on a leash, at your heels."

Camillo said, "Doing that would be good for her honor."

Flamineo said, "If you do these things, you would be certain in one fortnight, despite her chastity or innocence, to be cuckolded, which yet is in suspense."

Whether Camillo would or would not be cuckolded was in suspense because the future had not yet happened. Would he or wouldn't he be advised by Flamineo, his brother-in-law?

Flamineo said, "This is my counsel, and I ask no fee for it."

His advice was to NOT keep a close eye on Vittoria.

Camillo said, "Come, you don't know where my nightcap wrings me."

A nightcap would fit badly or not at all if worn by a horned cuckold.

Flamineo said, "Wear it in the old fashion; let your large ears come through — it will be more easy on your head."

The large ears he had in mind were those of an ass.

Flamineo continued, "I will be bitter — bar your wife from her entertainment: Women are more willingly and more gloriously chaste, when they are least restrained of their liberty."

His "bitterness" consisted of advising Camillo to keep a close eye on his wife and not allow her to enjoy entertainments.

Of course, he really wanted Camillo to give Vittoria her freedom so that Brachiano could make Camillo a cuckold.

Flamineo continued, "It seems that you would be a fine capricious, mathematically precise and jealous coxcomb and would measure the height of your own horns with a Jacob's staff even before they are up."

A Jacob's staff was used to make measurements.

Flamineo continued, "These politically cunning enclosures for paltry mutton create more rebellion in the flesh than all the provocative electuaries — aphrodisiacs — doctors have offered for sale since last jubilee."

"Mutton" was a slang term for prostitutes or sexually promiscuous women.

The "politically cunning enclosures" were the rooms in the house a wife would stay in while her husband refused to let her out of the house.

During a jubilee, people can buy indulgences that reduce after-death punishment for sins. For example, an indulgence can allow a repentant sinner to climb the Mountain of Purgatory more quickly. Some critics believed that people who paid money for indulgences were buying forgiveness for their sins.

Camillo said, "This does not help me —"

Flamineo said, "It seems you are jealous. I'll show you the error of it by a familiar example. I have seen a pair of spectacles fashioned with such perspective art, that if you lay down just one twelve-pence on the gambling table and look at it, it will appear as if there were twenty twelve-pence coins."

He was referring to trick eyeglasses that would make one object appear as twenty objects.

Flamineo continued, "If you were to wear a pair of these spectacles, and see your wife tying her shoe, you would imagine twenty hands were lifting up your wife's clothes, and this would put you into a horrible causeless fury."

Camillo said, "The fault there, sir, is not in the eyesight."

Flamineo said, "True, but they who have the yellow jaundice think all objects they look at are yellow.

"Jealousy is worse; her fits present to a man, like so many bubbles in a basin of water, twenty different crabbed faces; many times jealousy makes a man's own shadow his cuckold-maker."

A jealous man can look at his own shadow and think that the shadow is a man who has cuckolded him.

Vittoria Corombona — Camillo's wife and Flamineo's sister — entered the room. It was a large room, and she was some distance away.

Softly, Flamineo said, "Look, Vittoria is coming. What reason do you have to be jealous of this creature? What an ignorant ass or flattering knave might be accounted a man who would write sonnets to her eyes, or call her brow the snow of Mount Ida near Troy, or ivory of Corinth, or compare her hair to the blackbird's bill, when it is more similar to the blackbird's feather? This is all."

Flamineo was saying that Camillo had no real reason to be jealous of Vittoria, his wife. True, someone might write bad poetry to Vittoria but that bad poet would become known as an ignorant ass or a flattering knave. That was all Camillo need worry about.

In this society, fair skin was considered more beautiful than dark skin, and so the bad poet would praise a dark woman's skin by comparing it to snow or ivory.

The bad poet could make mistakes. The word "Corinth" was used to refer to a whorehouse, and the "ivory" could be interpreted as the ivory-white skin of the whores.

The bill of a blackbird is yellow, and the bad poet, to flatter a woman, might call her a blonde although her hair was black.

Flamineo continued, "Be wise; I will make you friends again with your wife, and you shall go to bed together. By the Virgin Mary — pay attention — it shall not be your seeking. *You* shall not be seen to seek to be reconciled with her. Insist upon that, by any means. Walk a little distance away, and be aloof. I would not have you be seen attempting to be reconciled to your wife."

Camillo walked a little distance away, but he could still hear Flamineo, unless he whispered — and he could hear Vittoria when she spoke.

Flamineo said to Vittoria, "Sister —"

He whispered to her, "My lord — Brachiano — will attend you in the banqueting-house."

The banqueting-house was a small building for meals in a garden. Affairs sometimes took place in banqueting-houses.

Flamineo continued, "— your husband is wondrously discontented."

Vittoria said, "I did nothing to displease him; I carved to him at supper-time."

She had shown respect to him by serving him.

Flamineo whispered to her, "You need not have carved him, in faith; they say he is a capon already."

A capon is a castrated cock (rooster). Figuratively, it is a eunuch.

Flamineo then whispered to her, "I must now seem to fall out and quarrel with you."

He said out loud so that both Camillo and Brachiano, who was hiding, could hear, "Shall a gentleman as well descended as Camillo —"

He whispered to Vittoria, "He is a lousy slave, who within these twenty years rode with the black guard in the duke's carriage, among spits and dripping-pans!"

Black guards were the lowest ranking menial workers in a kitchen.

Camillo said to himself, "Now he begins to tickle her."

The word "tickle" means "provoke" — it also means "arouse."

Flamineo said out loud, "— an excellent scholar —"

He whispered to Vittoria, "Camillo is a man who has a head filled with calves' brains without any sage in them."

As slang, the word "calf" meant a fool. "Sage" can mean 1) a herb, or 2) sagacity.

Flamineo continued, "— come crouching in the hams to you for a night's lodging?"

He whispered to Vittoria, "Camillo is a man who has an itch in his hams, which is like the fire at the glass-factory that has not gone out these past seven years."

An itch in the thighs can lessen the probability of having sex, especially when the itch is a symptom of a contagious disease. The word "fire" can mean "sexual passion."

Camillo had not had a sexual orgasm for the past seven years, according to Flamineo. If he had, the "fire" would have got out, at least briefly.

Flamineo asked out loud, "Isn't he a courtly gentleman?"

He whispered to Vittoria, "When he wears white satin, one would take him by his black muzzle to be no other creature than a maggot."

Maggots often have two dark spots at the posterior end.

Camillo's complexion was dark.

Flamineo said out loud, "You are a goodly foil, I confess. You are well set out."

A foil is a setting for a jewel such as a diamond. It is a thin piece of metal placed under the jewel to reflect light and enhance the jewel's brilliance.

He whispered to Vittoria, "But you are covered with a false stone — yonder counterfeit diamond."

A stallion "covers" a mare during sex. In slang, a "stone" is a testicle. Camillo was a counterfeit diamond because he lacked hardness.

Camillo said, "He will make her know what is in me."

Flamineo said out loud, "Come, my lord attends you; thou shall go to bed to my lord —"

Camillo thought that "my lord" was a flattering allusion to himself. Vittoria knew that Flamineo meant Brachiano.

Camillo said, "Now he comes to it."

Flamineo continued, "— with a relish as curious as a vintner going to taste new wine."

Vintners would be curious about the new wine: Is it good or bad?

Flamineo whispered to Camillo, "I am opening your case hard."

In law, "opening your case" meant pleading your case. As slang, the word "case" meant vagina. The word "hard" can refer to the state of a penis.

Camillo said to himself, "He is a virtuous brother, believe it!"

As Flamineo continued to speak, Camillo thought that Flamineo was talking about him (Camillo), but Vittoria knew that Flamineo was talking about Brachiano.

Flamineo said out loud, "He will give thee a ring with a philosopher's stone in it."

The philosopher's stone was reputed to turn base metal into precious metal. Alchemists attempted to create the stone. As slang, a "stone" is a testicle.

Camillo said to himself, "Indeed, I am studying alchemy."

Flamineo said out loud, "Thou shall lie in a bed stuffed with turtledoves' feathers; thou shall swoon in perfumed linen, like the fellow who was smothered in roses."

The young Roman emperor Elagabalus (203–222 C.E.) was reputed to have hosted a banquet during which petals fell from a false ceiling — so many petals fell that some of his guests were smothered to death. In 1888 the Anglo-Dutch artist Sir Lawrence Alma-Tadema painted this scene in his *The Roses of Heliogabalus*.

Flamineo continued, "So perfect shall be thy happiness, that as men at sea think land, and trees, and ships, go that way they go; so both heaven and earth shall seem to go your voyage."

Flamineo was incorrect. Land, and trees, and ships do not seem to go in the same direction the sailors are going. Imagine being on a train and looking out a window. The landscape as it goes past seems to be going in the opposite direction you are going; the landscape seems to be on the same journey you are on, but in reverse.

Flamineo was trying to say that Vittoria's happiness as she had an affair with Brachiano would be approved by heaven and earth, but the opposite was true. God and human morality do not approve of adultery.

Flamineo continued, "Thou shall meet him; it is affixed with nails of diamonds to inevitable necessity."

Nails made of diamond will last forever.

Vittoria whispered, "How shall we get rid of Camillo?"

Flamineo whispered to her, "I will put gadflies in his tail and set him gadding away soon."

He went over to Camillo and whispered, "I have almost brought her to it: She is almost ready to go to bed with you. I find her forthcoming, but if I might advise you now, for this night if I were you, I would not lie with her; instead, I would cross her humor to make her more humble."

Camillo whispered, "Shall I? Shall I?"

Flamineo whispered, "It will show in you a supremacy of judgment."

Camillo whispered, "True, and a mind differing from the tumultuary — irregular and haphazard — opinion; for, *quae negata, grata*."

The Latin words mean, "What is denied, is desired."

Flamineo whispered, "Right. You are the magnet that shall draw her to you, although you keep your distance from her."

Camillo whispered, "A philosophical — wise — reason."

Flamineo whispered, "Walk by her in the nobleman's fashion, and tell her you will lie with her at the end of the progress."

A progress is a state procession, as when a king traveled. In this case, Brachiano was visiting Camillo and staying overnight, and so Camillo would tell Vittoria that he would lie with her after Brachiano left the following day.

Camillo paraded in front of Vittoria and then said to her, "I cannot be induced, or as a man would say, incited —"

Vittoria interrupted, "To do what, sir?"

Camillo answered, "To lie with you tonight. Your silkworm used to fast every third day, and the following day it spins the better. Tomorrow at night, I am for you."

Actually, silkworms fast for two days and then spin for a few days without eating.

Vittoria said, "You'll spin a fair thread, trust to it."

The thread would be made of semen.

Flamineo said to Camillo, "But do you hear me? I think you shall steal to her bedchamber about midnight."

In other words: Camillo would not do as he said he would. Instead of refraining from lying with his wife this night, he would go to her around midnight.

Camillo asked, "Do you think so? Why, look, brother, because you shall not say I'll fool you and do what I said I would not do, take the key, lock me into the chamber, and say you shall be sure of me. You shall be sure that I don't go to my wife this night."

Flamineo said, "Truly I will do that. I'll be your jailor for this once."

Camillo said, "A pox on it, as I am a Christian! Tell me tomorrow how scurvily she takes my unkind parting."

"I will," Flamineo said.

"Didn't thou pay attention to the jest about the silkworm?" Camillo said. "Good night; indeed, I will use this trick often."

"Do, do, do," Flamineo said.

Camillo exited.

Flamineo locked the door.

Flamineo said to Vittoria, "So, now you are safe. Ha, ha, ha! Thou entangle thyself in thine own work like a silkworm."

Brachiano came out of hiding.

Flamineo said to Vittoria, "Come, sister, darkness hides your blush. Women are like cursed dogs. Civility keeps them tied all daytime, but they are let loose at midnight, and then they do the most good, or the most mischief."

Flamineo said to Brachiano, "My lord, my lord!"

Zanche, Vittoria's servant, brought out a carpet, spread it, and lay two fair cushions on it. She then stood near Flamineo.

Cornelia, Vittoria's mother, entered the room. She listened, but she remained unperceived.

Brachiano said, "Believe me, I could wish time would stand still and never end this interview, this hour. But all delight too soon devours itself."

He said to Vittoria, "Let me into your bosom, happy lady. Pour out, instead of eloquence, my vows. Loose and lose me not, madam, for if you forsake me, I am lost eternally."

To be lost eternally was to be damned to hell.

Vittoria replied, "Sir, in the way of pity, I wish you heart-whole."

"You are a sweet physician," Brachiano said.

Vittoria said, "Surely, sir, a loathed cruelty in ladies is like many funerals to doctors: It takes away their credit."

"Excellent creature!" Brachiano said. "We call the cruel fair; what name shall I have for you who are so merciful?"

"See now they close and come together," Zanche said.

"A very happy union," Flamineo said.

Cornelia, Vittoria's and Flamineo's mother, thought, *My fears have fallen upon me! What I feared is true! Oh, my heart! My son is a pander!*

Flamineo was pandering his sister to Brachiano. Pandering his sister to a powerful man could benefit Flamineo socially and financially.

Cornelia thought, *Now I find our family sinking to ruin. Earthquakes leave behind in existence, where they have tyrannized, iron, or lead, or stone. But — woe to those who are ruined! — violent lust leaves nothing behind.*

Brachiano fingered a jewel that Vittoria was wearing and asked, "Of what value is this jewel?"

A jewel is a symbol of married chastity: Think of a diamond wedding ring.

The ring itself symbolized a vagina; you can guess what the finger in the ring symbolizes.

A jewel can also be a sex organ, whether male or female.

Vittoria said, "It is the ornament of a weak fortune."

"In truth, I'll have it," Brachiano said. "I will just exchange my jewel for your jewel."

"Excellent," Flamineo said to himself. "His jewel for her jewel. Well put in, duke."

Indeed, the Duke of Brachiano wanted his "jewel" well put in Vittoria's "jewel."

Brachiano and Vittoria exchanged literal jewels.

Brachiano said, "Let me see you wear it."

Vittoria positioned the jewel at the top of her bodice and asked, "Here, sir?"

Brachiano replied, "No, lower, you shall wear my jewel lower."

Flamineo said, "That's better: She must wear his jewel lower."

If the jewel were positioned at the bottom of her bodice, it would to her *mons Veneris*, aka *mons pubis*.

Vittoria said, "To pass away the time, I'll tell your grace a dream I had last night."

"I very much wish to hear about it," Brachiano said.

Vittoria said, "It is a foolish idle dream.

"I thought I walked about the middle of night into a churchyard, where a well-grown yew-tree spread her large root in ground."

As will become clear, at least sometimes the "yew-tree" is a "you-tree" — that it, it symbolizes Brachiano. Vittoria's image of the yew-tree's root spreading in ground is a sexual image.

Vittoria continued, "Under that yew, as I sat sadly leaning on a grave, checkered with cross-sticks" — placed on the tombstone in a pattern forming a checkerboard were witches' cross-sticks that were used to raise storms — "there came stealing in your duchess-wife and my husband; one of them bore a pickaxe and the other bore a rusty spade, and in rough terms they began to challenge me about this yew."

"That tree?" Brachiano asked.

Vittoria replied, "This harmless yew. They told me my intent was to root up that well-grown yew and plant in the stead of it a withered blackthorn, and for that they vowed to bury me alive."

The well-grown yew, in the opinion of Brachiano's duchess (Isabella) and Vittoria's husband, was Vittoria's husband: Camillo. And in their opinion, the withered blackthorn was Brachiano.

In Vittoria's opinion, the well-grown yew (you) was Brachiano. And in her opinion, the withered blackthorn was Camillo.

Vittoria continued, "My husband immediately with a pickaxe began to dig, and your deadly duchess with a shovel, like a Fury — a goddess of vengeance — emptied out the earth and scattered bones.

"Lord, how I thought I trembled, and yet for all this terror I could not pray."

Flamineo said, "No; the devil was in your dream."

Vittoria said, "When to my rescue there arose, I thought, a whirlwind, which let fall a massive arm from that strong tree; and both were struck dead by that sacred yew in that base shallow grave that was their due."

"Excellent devil!" Flamineo said. "She has taught him in a dream to make away his duchess and her husband."

To Flamineo, Vittoria's recounting of her dream was a coded message to Brachiano, telling him to murder his wife and her husband.

Brachiano put his arms around her and said, "Sweetly shall I interpret this your dream. You are lodged within the arms of him who shall protect you from all the fevers of a jealous husband and from the poor envy of our phlegmatic — dull — duchess.

"I'll seat you above law, and above scandal. I'll give to your thoughts the invention of delight and the fruition. Nor shall government divide me from you longer than a care to keep you great. You shall to me at once be dukedom, health, wife, children, friends, and all."

He would attend to governing only so that he could make and keep Vittoria a great lady. Other than that, he would ignore governing so that he could spend more time with her.

Cornelia, who was Vittoria's and Flamineo's mother, came forward and revealed herself, saying, "Woe to light hearts; they always come before our fall!"

Flamineo said to her, "What Fury raised thee up?"

He then said to Zanche, Vittoria's servant, "Leave! Leave!"

He did not want her to witness what would follow.

She exited.

Cornelia said to Brachiano, "What are you doing here, my lord, this dead of night? Mildew never dropped on a flower here until now."

Flamineo said, "Please, will you go to bed then, lest you be blasted?"

Cornelia said, "Oh, that this fair garden had with all the poisoned herbs of Thessaly at first been planted and made a nursery for witchcraft, rather than be made a burial plot for both your honors!"

Medea, the witch who married Jason and later killed their children, was reputed to have taken her poisonous herbs with her to Thessaly.

Vittoria knelt and said, "Dearest mother, hear what I have to say."

Cornelia replied, "Oh, thou make my brow bend to the earth sooner than nature! See the curse of children! In life they keep us frequently in tears, and in the cold grave they leave us in pale fears."

Brachiano said to her, "Come, come, I will not listen to you."

Vittoria began, "My dear lord —"

Cornelia interrupted, "Where is thy duchess now, adulterous duke? Thou little dream that this night she has come to Rome."

Flamineo said, "What! Come to Rome!"

Vittoria said, "The duchess!"

Brachiano began, "She would have been better —"

Cornelia interrupted, "The lives of princes should move like dials, whose regular example is so strong that they make the times by them go right, or wrong."

The word 'dial' meant sundial or clock. It is a guide to the correct time.

Princes can make the times go right or go wrong. It is better if they are ideal rulers and make the times go right.

Antonio de Guevara's book *The Dial of Princes* was about Marcus Aurelius, an ideal prince. The book was a guide to the characteristics of a good ruler.

Flamineo asked, "So, have you finished?"

Cornelia said, "Unfortunate Camillo!"

Vittoria said, "I protest, if any chaste denial, if anything but blood could have allayed his long suit to me —"

"Blood" can mean 1) sexual passion, 2) life-blood, and/or 3) bloodshed.

"His long suit" meant Brachiano's long pursuit of her. He would not accept a chaste denial, and so the alternatives were sexual passion (sleeping with him), life-blood (either Vittoria or Brachiano or both would die, and bloodshed (Brachiano could kill his wife and Vittorio's husband).

Cornelia knelt beside Vittoria and said, "I will join with thee, kneeling to the most woeful end a mother ever kneeled."

The most woeful end is eternal damnation, which can be one's doom on the Day of Judgment if one commits the sin of adultery and dies without sincerely repenting that sin. Kneeling and praying for the strength not to commit that sin is better than committing the sin and then repenting.

Cornelia said to her daughter, "If thou dishonor thus thy husband's bed, may thy life be as short as are the funeral tears in great men's —"

What would follow? The word "eyes"?

Would Brachiano mourn Vittoria if she were to die? Do great men mourn the women they corrupt? According to Cornelia, he would mourn, or pretend to mourn, but not for long.

Or would what would follow be "mourners' eyes"?

When a great man dies, often mourners will put on a brief show of mourning although they may actually be glad the great man died.

Brachiano interrupted, "Bah, bah, the woman's mad."

Cornelia said to him, "Let thy act be Judas-like; betray in kissing."

She then said to Vittoria, "May thou be envied during his short breath, and pitied like a wretch after his death!"

Vittoria said, "Oh, I am accursed!"

She rose and exited.

Cornelia rose.

Flamineo asked, "Are you out of your wits?"

As he said this, he was looking in between Brachiano and the door through which Vittoria had exited. He was angry at both Brachiano (for letting Vittoria leave) and at Vittoria (for leaving), but he did not want the Duke of Brachiano, a powerful man, to know how angry at him he was. He was also angry at Cornelia.

Flamineo said to Brachiano, "My lord, I'll fetch her back again."

Brachiano replied, "No, I'll go to bed. Send Doctor Julio to me soon."

He then said to Cornelia, "Uncharitable woman! Thy rash tongue has raised a fearful and prodigious storm. Be thou the cause of all ensuing harm."

Brachiano exited.

Flamineo and his mother, Cornelia, were alone.

Flamineo said to his mother, "Now, you who stand so much upon your honor, is this a fitting time of night, do you think, to send a duke home without a manservant to attend him? I would like to know where lies the mass of wealth that you have hoarded for my maintenance, so that I may bear my beard out of the level of my lord's stirrup."

A lord's footmen ran while the lord rode a horse. A footman's beard would be — Flamineo said — at the level of the lord's stirrup. Of course, the footman would likely have to bow for that to be true.

Cornelia said, "What! Shall we be vicious because we are poor?"

Was poverty a good reason for Flamineo to pander his sister to the Duke of Brachiano?

Flamineo said, "Please, what means do you have to keep me from the galleys or from the gallows?"

Many impoverished people committed crimes to support themselves, were caught, and were sentenced either to row in a galley ship or to be hung.

He continued, "My father proved himself a gentleman, sold all his land, and, like a fortunate fellow, died before the money was spent.

"You brought me up at Padua, I confess, where I say, for lack of means — the University of Padua judge me — I have been obliged to heel at my tutor's stockings, at least seven years; conspiring with a beard made me a graduate; then I went into this duke's service and visited the court, from which I returned more courteous and more lecherous by far, but not a suit the richer."

Impoverished students at universities could earn their keep and education by acting as servants to their tutors.

Flamineo may not have been a good student since he had to conspire with a beard — perhaps by performing special favors for the elderly professor — to get his degree.

"Courteous" means "well-mannered" and "like a courtier." Some courtiers are corrupt.

By "suit" Flamineo may have meant a suit of clothing, or he may have meant a petition that would make him better off socially and financially.

He continued, "And shall I, having a path so open, and so free to my advancement in society, still retain your milk in my pale forehead?"

Flamineo regarded following his mother's sense of morality as equivalent to being a mama's boy and having a pale, pasty complexion.

He continued, "No, this face of mine I'll arm and fortify with lusty wine against shame and blushing."

After drinking a few glasses of wine, he would feel no blame and would not blush.

Flamineo was wrong about many things, including not blushing in this situation. Drinking too much alcohol causes facial flushing.

Cornelia said, "Oh, I wish that I had never given birth to thee!"

"So wish I," Flamineo said. "I wish that the most common courtesan in Rome had been my mother, rather than thyself. Nature shows much pity to whores, to give them only few children, yet give those children a plurality of fathers; those children are sure that they shall not want."

This is not likely for the children of a common courtesan. For the mistress of a king, perhaps.

He continued, "Go, go, complain to my great lord Cardinal Monticelso. It may be that he will justify the act."

The act was the act of pandering his sister to the Duke of Brachiano.

Flamineo continued, "Lycurgus wondered much why men would provide good stallions for their mares, and yet would allow their fair wives to be barren."

Flamineo's understanding of the Spartan King Lycurgus was at best partially right. Lycurgus believed in eugenics, and so a husband ought to be happy if a better man than he would make his wife pregnant.

In many societies, but not in ancient Sparta, a rich man is often considered to be a better man than an impoverished man.

Cornelia said, "Misery of miseries!"

She exited.

Alone, Flamineo said, "The Duchess of Brachiano has come to court! I don't like that.

"We are engaged to do mischief, and must continue on.

"We see rivers find the ocean with the river's crooked bendings beneath forced, made-by-violence banks.

"We see, to aspire some mountain's top, the way ascends not straight, but imitates the subtle foldings of a winter's snake.

"Just like those things, whoever knows policy and her true aspect shall find her ways winding and indirect."

Once again, Flamineo was only partially correct. Snakes certainly can make foldings with their bodies, but during a cold winter snakes become dormant and any foldings they make are not subtle — a word that means shrewd, wise, and discerning.

He had previously been at best partially correct about the care fathers give to the children of prostitutes and about Lycurgus' beliefs concerning fathers.

He was also only partially correct about ambition. Yes, it is good to try to better one's position in society, but no, it is not good to do so by pandering one's sister.

CHAPTER 2

— 2.1 —

Francisco de Medici, Cardinal Monticelso, Marcello, Isabella, young Giovanni, and young Jacques the Moor were in a room together.

Francisco de Medici was the Duke of Florence.

Marcello was an attendant of the Duke of Florence, and he was the brother of Flamineo and Vittoria.

Isabella was the Duke of Brachiano's wife, and young Giovanni was their son. Isabella was also the sister of Francisco de Medici, and so young Giovanni was his nephew.

Young Jacques the Moor was an attendant of young Giovanni.

Francisco de Medici asked Isabella, "Haven't you seen your husband since you arrived?"

"Not yet, sir," Isabella answered.

Francisco de Medici said, "Surely he is wondrously kind. If I had such a dove-house as Camillo's, I would set it on fire if only to destroy the polecats that haunt it."

The "dove" in Camillo's dove-house was his wife, Vittoria. Brachiano was one of the "polecats" who haunted Camillo's dove-house.

Brachiano was "wondrously kind" because he did not set the dove-house on fire.

Francisco de Medici and Isabella had heard about the Duke of Brachiano's desire to have an affair with Camillo's wife, Vittoria.

Young Giovanni came over to Francisco de Medici, who said, "My sweet nephew!"

Young Giovanni said, "Lord uncle, you promised me a horse and armor."

Francisco de Medici replied, "That I did, my pretty nephew."

He then ordered, "Marcello, see that young Giovanni gets a horse and armor."

Marcello said, "My lord, the Duke of Brachiano is here."

Francisco de Medici said to Isabella, "Sister, leave; you must not yet be seen."

Isabella, a good and forgiving wife, replied, "I ask you to entreat him mildly. Don't let your rough tongue set us at louder variance; all the wrongs he committed against me are freely pardoned, and I do not doubt that, as men to test the precious unicorn's horn make of the powder a preservative circle, and in it put a spider, so these arms shall charm his poison, force it to be obeying, and keep him chaste from an infected straying."

Francisco de Medici replied, "I wish that the circle of your arms may do that."

The unicorn's horn was believed to be an antidote to poison. To test whether a powder was genuine powdered unicorn's horn, some of the powder was used to make a circle, and a spider — spiders were thought to be poisonous — was placed in the circle. If the spider left the circle, the powder was not an effective antidote against poison and so it was not genuine powdered unicorn horn.

Francisco de Medici then said to his sister, "Leave."

Isabella exited as Brachiano and Flamineo entered the scene.

Francisco de Medici ordered, "Void the chamber."

Everyone left except for Francisco de Medici, Brachiano, and Cardinal Monticelso. Francisco de Medici was Brachiano's brother-in-law. Cardinal Monticelso was the uncle of Camillo, who was the husband of Vittoria, with whom Brachiano was in love.

Francisco de Medici said to Brachiano, "You are welcome; will you sit?"

He then said to Cardinal Monticelso, "Please, my lord, be my orator and speak for me — my heart's too full. I'll second you soon and support what you say."

Cardinal Monticelso said to Brachiano, "Before I begin, let me entreat your grace to forgo all passion — all violent emotion — which may be raised by my free discourse."

Brachiano replied, "I will be as silent as in the church. You may proceed."

Cardinal Monticelso said, "It is a wonder to your noble friends, that you, having as it were entered the world with a free scepter in your able hand, and having well applied high gifts of learning to the use of your natural gifts, should in your prime age neglect your awe-inspiring throne for the soft down of an insatiate bed."

As a duke, Brachiano ought to be applying himself to ruling well; instead, he was pursuing another man's wife.

Cardinal Monticelso continued, "Oh, my lord, the drunkard after all his lavish cups is dry, and then is sober; so at length, when you awake from this lascivious dream, repentance then will follow, like the sting placed in the adder's tail."

Alcohol causes urination and depletes the body of water, and then the body grows sober.

Sinning may feel good, but like an alcoholic waking up with a headache, the sinner can wake up with a feeling of repentance, which can sting like the bite of an adder.

In this society, people believed that adders had a sting in their tail.

Cardinal Monticelso continued, "Wretched are princes when fortune blasts just a petty flower of their unwieldy crowns, or ravishes just one pearl from their scepter."

He was wittily punning. A flower can be a jewel in a crown, and a crown can be a garland of flowers.

He continued, "But alas! When they to willful shipwreck lose good reputation, all princely titles — ranks, possessions, rights — perish with their name."

Brachiano began, "You have said, my lord —"

Cardinal Monticelso interrupted, "— enough to give you a taste of how far I am from flattering your greatness."

Brachiano said to Francisco de Medici, "Now you who are his second, what do you say?"

A second is a supporter. Francisco de Medici supported what Cardinal Monticelso was saying to Brachiano.

Brachiano continued, "Don't act like young hawks that fetch a course about. Your game flies fair, and for you."

A young hawk might be afraid to attack certain game and so would turn back. Brachiano was saying that Francisco de Medici and Cardinal Monticelso ought not to be afraid to attack him. This did not imply that he would not respond to their attack.

Francisco de Medici said, "Do not fear that we will be afraid to speak frankly to you. I'll answer you in your own hawking phraseology.

"Some eagles that should gaze upon the sun seldom soar high, but take their lustful ease, since they from dunghill birds their prey can seize."

Eagles were reputed to be the only birds that could stare at the sun. Brachiano was a metaphorical eagle that did not soar high and did not attack valuable game, but instead attacked prey of little worth — he pursued another man's wife.

Francisco de Medici asked, "Do you know Vittoria?"

Brachiano replied, "Yes."

Francisco de Medici asked, "Do you change your shirt there, when you retire from playing tennis?"

Brachiano replied, "Happily."

In this society, the word was ambiguous and could also mean "haply," or "perhaps."

Francisco de Medici said, "Her husband is the lord of a poor fortune, yet she wears expensive cloth of tissue."

"So what?" Brachiano said. "Will you urge that, my good lord Cardinal Monticelso, as part of her shrift at next confession, and know from whence it sails?"

By "from whence it sails," he meant "from where she got it."

Francisco de Medici began, "She is your strumpet —"

Brachiano replied, "Uncivil sir, there's hemlock — poison — in thy breath and that black slander. If she were a whore of mine, all thy loud cannons, thy Swiss mercenaries, thy galleys, and thy sworn confederates would not dare to overthrow her."

Francisco de Medici said, "Let's not talk about thunder. Thou have a wife, our sister; I wish that I had given both her white hands to death, bound and locked fast in her final winding — funeral — sheet, when I gave thee but one of her hands in marriage."

A winding-sheet is a shroud.

Brachiano said, "Thou had given a soul to God then."

"True, in her case," Francisco de Medici said. "Thy ghostly father — your father confessor — with all his absolution, his power to forgive sins, shall never do so by thee."

"Spit thy poison," Brachiano replied.

"I shall not need to," Francisco de Medici said. "Lust carries her sharp whip at her own girdle. Look to it, for our anger is making thunderbolts."

He was angry.

"Thunder!" Brachiano said. "Indeed, the thunderbolts are only firecrackers."

Francisco de Medici said, "We'll end this with the cannon."

Brachiano said, "Thou shall get nothing by it, except iron in thy wounds and gunpowder in thy nostrils."

Francisco de Medici said, "Better that than to exchange perfumes for plasters."

The perfumes were accessories to lustful desire, while the plasters — bandages — were accessories to the treatment of venereal disease caused by lustful desire.

Brachiano said, "Pity on thee! It would be good if you'd show your slaves or condemned men your new-plowed forehead."

Francisco de Medici's forehead was furrowed with anger.

Brachiano said, "Defiance! I'll meet thee, even in a thicket of thy ablest men."

He was willing to fight Francisco de Medici — and his ablest men.

Cardinal Monticelso said, "My lords, you shall not word it any further without a milder limit."

Francisco de Medici and Brachiano were becoming too angry at each other.

Francisco de Medici replied, "Willingly."

Brachiano asked, "Have you proclaimed a triumph? Is that why you bait a lion like this?"

The lion was Brachiano, and to Brachiano it was as if Francisco de Medici had proclaimed a triumph — a public festival in which part of the entertainment was having dogs bait — torment — a lion so it would fight.

Cardinal Monticelso said, "My lord!"

Calming down a little, Brachiano said, "I am tame. I am tame, sir."

In this society, Catholic cardinals were respected.

Francisco de Medici said a sonnet — in this case, a short non-rhyming poem:

"We send to the duke for a conference

"About levies against the pirates; my lord duke

"Is not at home: We come ourself in person;
"Still my lord duke is busy. But we fear that
"When the Tiber River to each prowling passerby
"Reveals flocks of wild ducks, then, my lord —
"About molting time I mean — we shall be certain
"To find you sure enough, and speak with you."

Brachiano said, "Ha!"

Francisco de Medici replied, "This is a mere tale of a tub — a mere cock-and-bull story. My words are idle. But to express the sonnet clearly, when stags grow melancholic you'll find the season."

Francisco de Medici, who was the Duke of Florence, was saying that he had come to the Duke of Brachiano because pirates were becoming a problem. Brachiano, however, was busy because of "wild ducks" — slang for whores. During the molting season, wild ducks lost feathers; men infected with syphilis after consorting with "wild ducks" lost their hair. However, just as stags were believed to grow melancholic and depart from the herd after rutting, Brachiano would grow melancholic because of venereal disease and finally would ignore his whore and attend to the business of governing.

Young Giovanni, wearing the armor given to him by his uncle, Francisco de Medici, entered the scene.

Cardinal Monticelso said, "No more, my lord; here comes a champion who shall end the difference between the two of you: your son, the Prince Giovanni. See, my lords, what hopes you store in him; this is a casket for both your crowns, and should be held likewise dear."

Giovanni could inherit both of their crowns. He was the Duke of Brachiano's son, and since the Duke of Florence had no children, his nephew could inherit his crown.

Cardinal Monticelso said, "Now is he apt for acquiring knowledge; therefore, know it is a more direct and even way to train to virtue those of princely blood by examples than by precepts, by actions rather than words. If he acquires knowledge by examples, whom should he rather strive to imitate than his own father?

"Brachiano, be his pattern — his good example — then. Leave him a stock of virtue that may last, even if bad fortune tears his sails and splits his mast."

Brachiano said, "Give me your hand, boy. Are you growing to be a soldier?"

Young Giovanni replied, "Give me a pike."

A pike is a weapon; it is a staff with a point.

Francisco de Medici joked, "What, practicing your pike so young, fair nephew?"

The joke was that a pike is a symbol for a penis.

Young Giovanni replied, "Suppose me one of Homer's frogs, my lord, tossing my bulrush thus."

He pretended to throw a pike.

In *The Battle of Frogs and Mice*, a mock-epic then attributed to Homer, frogs used bulrushes as pikes.

Young Giovanni continued, "Please, sir, tell me, mightn't a child of good discretion be the leader of an army?"

"Discretion" meant the ability to act on one's own.

Francisco de Medici replied, "Yes, nephew, a young prince of good discretion might."

According to Falstaff in William Shakespeare's *1 Henry IV*, "Discretion is the better part of valor." Falstaff's discretion was to stay out of harm's way and let others do the fighting.

Young Giovanni replied, "Do you say so?

"Indeed I have heard that it is fitting that a general should not often endanger his own person, as long as he makes a noise when he's on horseback like a Danish drummer — oh, Danish martial music is excellent! As long as he does that, he need not fight! I think his horse might lead an army for him as well as he can.

"If I live to grow up, I'll charge the French foe in the very front of all my troops, the foremost man."

Francisco de Medici said, "What! What!"

Young Giovanni continued, "And I will not bid my soldiers to go up to the front and then I will follow them — but instead I'll bid them to follow me."

Brachiano said, "Forward lapwing! He flies with the shell on his head."

Lapwings were precocious, and so was young Giovanni. Lapwings were birds that were thought to be able to run immediately after hatching — with part of its shell still on its head. Young Giovanni was so precocious that he could fly — not just run — with part of the shell still on his head.

Francisco de Medici said, "Pretty nephew!"

Young Giovanni said, "The first year, uncle, that I go to war, all prisoners that I take, I will set free without their ransom."

Francisco de Medici said, "Ha! Without their ransom! How then will you reward your soldiers, who captured those prisoners for you?"

Young Giovanni said, "This way, my lord: I'll marry them to all the wealthy widows of those soldiers who fall that year."

Francisco de Medici said, "Why then, the next year following, you'll have no men to go with you to war."

The men would be needed at home to take care of their wives and babies.

Giovanni said, "Why then I'll draft the women to go to the war, and then the men will follow."

Cardinal Monticelso said, "Witty prince!"

Francisco de Medici said, "See, a good habit makes a child a man, whereas a bad one makes a man a beast."

A good "habit" — clothing or costume such as a suit of armor — makes a child a man.

A bad "habit" — way of acting — makes a man a beast.

He then said to Brachiano, "Come, you and I are friends."

Brachiano replied, "Most wishedly. Like bones that, broke in two, and well set, knit the more strongly."

Francisco de Medici ordered an attendant, "Call Camillo hither."

He then said to Brachiano, "You have heard the rumor that Count Lodovico has turned into a pirate?"

Lodovico had earlier been banished.

Brachiano replied, "Yes."

Francisco de Medici said, "We are now preparing to fetch him in."

Isabella entered the room.

Seeing her, Francisco de Medici said, "Behold your duchess. We now will leave you, and we expect from you nothing but kind entreaty."

The word "entreaty" meant negotiations.

Brachiano replied, "You have charmed me."

Francisco de Medici, Cardinal Monticelso, and young Giovanni exited, leaving the Duke of Brachiano and Isabella, his duchess, alone.

Using the majestic plural, Brachiano said to her, "You are in health, we see."

Isabella replied, "And above health, because I see that my lord is well."

In this society, wives called their husband "lord."

Brachiano replied, "So, I wonder much what amorous whirlwind hurried you to Rome."

This was an accusation of infidelity.

Isabella replied, "Devotion, my lord."

She meant devotion to her husband.

Deliberating misunderstanding her to mean religious devotion, Brachiano said, "Devotion! Is your soul charged with any grievous sin?"

Isabella said, "It is burdened with too many; and I think that the oftener we cast our reckonings up, our sleep will be the sounder."

Brachiano said, "Go to your bedchamber."

Isabella said, "Nay, my dear lord, I will not have you angry! Doesn't my absence from you, now two months, merit one kiss?"

"I am not accustomed to kiss," Brachiano said. "If that will dispossess your jealousy, I'll swear it to you."

Isabella replied, "Oh, my beloved lord, I do not come to chide you — my jealousy! I have yet to learn what that Italian means."

The Italians were believed to get jealous easily.

Isabella said, "You are as welcome to these longing arms, as I was welcome to you as a virgin."

Brachiano replied, "Oh, your breath! Damn sweet foods and the continued use of medicine — the plague is in them!"

Isabella said, "You have often, for these two lips, neglected the perfume cassia, or the natural sweets of the spring-violet. My two lips are not yet much withered.

"My lord, I should be merry.

"Your frowns are lovely and appropriate in a helmet; but when you frown at me, in such a peaceful interview, I think your brows are too, too roughly knit."

"Oh, dissemblance!" Brachiano said. "Do you raise and band together factions against me? Have you learned the trick of impudent baseness to complain to your kindred?"

Isabella's brother was Francisco de Medici, the Duke of Florence.

Isabella replied, "Never, my dear lord."

Brachiano said, "Must I be hunted out? Or was it your trick to meet some amorous gallant here in Rome, an amorous gallant who must replace me?"

Isabella said, "Please, sir, burst my heart; and in my death return to your former pity and kind feelings for me, though not love for me."

Brachiano said, "Because your brother is the corpulent duke — that is, the great duke — damn it, I shall not shortly gamble away five hundred crowns wagering at tennis, but it shall be recorded and held against me! I scorn him like I scorn a head-shaven Polack who lacks respect for human life. All his reverend intelligence lies in his wardrobe; he's a discreet fellow — when he's made up in his robes of state.

"Your brother, the great duke, because he has galleys, and now and then ransacks a fast Turkish fly-boat — may now all the hellish Furies take his soul! — first made this marriage match. Cursed be the priest who sang the wedding-mass, and cursed even be my son!"

Isabella said, "Oh, too, too far you have cursed!"

Brachiano said, "Your hand I'll kiss."

He kissed her hand and said, "This is the last ceremony of my love. Henceforth I'll never lie with thee — by this, this wedding-ring, I swear that I'll never more lie with thee! And this divorce shall be as truly kept as if the judge had made this divorce a legal judgment! Fare you well. Our sleeps are severed. We will never again sleep together."

He was divorcing her from his bed.

Isabella said, "You would forbid it the sweet union of all things blessed! Why, the saints in heaven will knit their brows at that."

Brachiano said, "Don't let thy love make thee an unbeliever of what I say; this my vow shall never, on my soul, be satisfied with my repentance — let thy brother rage with a violence beyond a horrid tempest or a sea-fight. My vow is fixed."

Isabella said, "Oh, my winding-sheet — my shroud! Now I shall need thee shortly."

She continued, "My dear lord, let me hear, once more, what I do not wish to hear: Never?"

Brachiano replied, "Never."

Isabella said, "Oh, my unkind lord! May your sins find mercy, as I upon a woeful widowed bed shall pray for you, if not to turn your eyes upon your wretched wife and hopeful son, yet I shall pray that in time you'll fix them upon heaven!"

"No more," Brachiano said. "Go, go, complain to the great duke, your brother."

"No, my dear lord," Isabella said. "You shall have immediate witness of how I'll work peace between you and my brother. I will make myself the author of your cursed vow. I have some cause to do it — you have none."

Isabella was going to take the blame for the divorce. That way, her brother would be angry at her, not at her husband. She had not committed adultery, and so he did not have that reason to divorce her. She knew that her husband was pursuing a married woman, and so she had that reason to divorce him. She could say that their separation was because of jealousy, and her brother and the cardinal would believe her. In this society, divorce was a serious undertaking, and both her brother and the cardinal would oppose it.

She continued, "Conceal, I beg you, for the good of both your dukedoms, that you wrought the means of such a separation."

The two dukedoms were of Brachiano and, through Isabella, of Florence. Brachiano was a member of the Ursini family, while Isabella was a member of the Medici family.

She continued, "Let the fault remain with my supposed jealousy, and think with what a piteous and rent heart I shall perform this sad ensuing part."

Francisco de Medici, Cardinal Monticelso, Flamineo, and Marcello entered the room.

Marcello was an attendant of the Duke of Florence, and he was the brother of Flamineo and Vittoria.

Flamineo was the secretary of Brachiano, and he was the brother of Marcello and Vittoria.

Brachiano said to Isabella, "Well, take your course."

He then said, "My honorable brother-in-law!"

Francisco de Medici said, "Sister!"

Isabella was crying.

Francisco de Medici said to Brachiano, "This is not well, my lord."

He then said, "Why, sister!"

Knowing that her meeting with her husband had not gone well, he said, "She does not deserve this welcome."

Brachiano said, "Welcome, you say! She has given me a sharp welcome!"

He was blaming her for a bad welcome.

Francisco de Medici said to his sister, "Are you foolish? Come, dry your tears. Is this a modest course to better what is wicked — to rail and weep? Grow to a reconciliation, or, by heaven, I'll never more deal between you."

"Sir, you shall not," Isabella said. "No, even if Vittoria, upon that condition, would become chaste."

Francisco de Medici asked, "Was your husband loud since we departed?"

He was asking if Brachiano had shouted at her.

Isabella said, "By my life, sir, no, I swear by that I do not care to lose."

She did not care to lose her honesty and chastity. She also did not care to lose eternal life in Paradise.

Isabella continued, "Are all these ruins of my former beauty laid out for a whore's triumph?"

The "whore" was Vittoria.

Francisco de Medici said, "Listen to me. Look at other women and see with what patience they suffer these slight wrongs, and with what justice they take pains to requite them. Take that course and do what they do."

Isabella said, "Oh, I wish that I were a man, or that I had the power to execute my fully understood wishes! I would whip some with scorpions."

A scorpion was a special kind of whip with knotted cords, plummets of lead, or steel spikes; it was used to inflict severe pain.

1 Kings 12.11 uses the word "scorpions" figuratively: "*And now whereas my father did lade you with a heavy yoke, I will add to your yoke: my father hath chastised you with whips, but I will chastise you with scorpions*" (King James Bible).

So does 2 Chronicles 10.11: "*For whereas my father put a heavy yoke upon you, I will put more to your yoke: my father chastised you with whips, but I will chastise you with scorpions*" (King James Bible).

Francisco de Medici said, "What! Turned into a Fury!"

Isabella said, "I want to dig that strumpet's eyes out; let her lie some twenty months a-dying. I want to cut off her nose and lips. I want to pull out her rotten teeth. I want to preserve her flesh like a mummy. I want these things to be trophies of my just anger! Hell, compared to my affliction, is mere snow-water."

She said to her husband, "By your favor, sir — brother, draw near, and my lord cardinal — by your favor, sir, let me borrow of you just one kiss. Henceforth I'll never lie with you, I swear by this, this wedding-ring."

Francisco de Medici said, "What! Never more lie with him!"

Isabella said, "And this divorce shall be as truly kept as if in a thronged court a thousand ears had heard it, and a thousand lawyers' hands had sealed and made legal the separation."

Brachiano said, "Never lie with me!"

Isabella replied, "Don't let my former dotage — doting love — for you make thee an unbeliever; this my vow shall never on my soul be satisfied with my repentance: *manet alta mente repostum*."

The Latin meant: "It remains stored in [my] deep mind."

The word "It" was ambiguous: Did it refer to her dotage or to her new vow?

The Latin passage came from Virgil's *Aeneid*, Book I, line 26. There it refers to Juno's remembering in the depths of her mind the Judgment of Paris, in which Prince Paris of Troy chose Venus as the most beautiful goddess instead of Juno or Minerva. Because of this, Juno hated all Trojans, including Aeneas, and did all she could to conquer Troy and to keep Aeneas from reaching Italy and becoming an important ancestor of the Roman people.

Francisco de Medici said, "Now, I swear by my birth, you are a foolish, mad, and jealous woman."

The hypocritical Brachiano said, "You see that this divorce is not what I wanted."

Francisco de Medici said to his sister, "Was this your circle of pure unicorn's horn that you said would charm your lord!"

He added, "Now horns upon thee, for jealousy deserves them!"

In other words: You deserve your husband to be unfaithful. You deserve to be a female cuckold.

He then said, "Keep your vow and take your bedchamber."

In other words: Keep your marriage vow and sleep with your husband.

Isabella replied, "No, sir, I'll go immediately to Padua. I will not stay a minute longer here."

Cardinal Monticelso said, "Oh, good madam!"

Brachiano said, "It would be best to let her have what she wants. Some half-day's journey will bring down her pride, and then she'll turn around and return post-haste."

Francisco de Medici said, "To see her come back to my lord Brachiano for a dispensation of her rash vow will beget excellent laughter."

Isabella recited a common proverb to herself:

"Unkindness, do thy office; poor heart, break:

"Those are the killing griefs, which dare not speak."

Another, similar proverb stated, "Grief pent up will break the heart."

She exited.

Camillo entered the room.

Marcello said to Francisco de Medici, "Camillo's come, my lord."

Francisco de Medici asked, "Where's the commission?"

He was going to give Camillo a commission to do a job.

Marcello answered, "Here it is."

Francisco de Medici said, "Give me the signet ring."

Francisco de Medici and Camillo began to talk together.

Flamineo led Brachiano to the side and said to him about Francisco de Medici and Camillo, "My lord, do you notice their whispering? I will compound a medicine out of their two heads, stronger than garlic, deadlier than poisonous metallic antimony."

Flamineo wanted both Francisco de Medici and Camillo to be dead. Their deaths would be like a medicine to him.

Flamineo continued, "The cantharides — a species of blister beetle known as Spanish fly — which are scarcely seen to stick upon the flesh, when they work to the heart, shall not do it with more silence or invisible cunning."

Spanish fly can be poisonous if used ill-advisedly. Flamineo believed that if Spanish fly were applied to the skin, it would work its way to the heart.

Flamineo was going to concoct a poison.

Brachiano said, "Tell me about the murder."

Flamineo said, "They are sending Camillo to Naples, but I'll send him to Candy."

Candy is Crete. Sending someone to Candy was a euphemism for sending someone to their death because the inhabitants of Candy were thought to eat poisonous snakes, a dangerous food to catch.

Doctor Julio entered the room.

Seeing Doctor Julio, Flamineo said, "Here's another property, too."

It was as if Flamineo were creating a play, and the doctor was a theatrical prop.

Brachiano said, "Oh, the doctor!"

Doctor Julio came over to them.

Flamineo said, "This doctor is a poor quack-salving knave, my lord; he is one who would have been lashed for his lechery, except that he confessed a judgment, had an execution laid upon him, and so put the whip to a non plus."

Doctor Julio added, "And I was cozened, my lord, by an arranter knave than myself, and made to pay all the colorable execution."

Doctor Julio should have been whipped for lechery, but he said that he had already been convicted on account of a debt he owed. He was taken into custody and so got out of the whipping, but another, more arrant knave than he was said that he was the man to whom the doctor owed the money (although no such debt actually existed). Doctor Julio was forced to pay the knave money.

Flamineo said, "He who will shoot pills into a man's guts shall make the man have more vents than a cornet or a lamprey."

In this society, cornets were wind instruments with many holes. Lampreys were fish with many apertures on their heads to allow water to flow over their gills.

Flamineo continued, "He will poison a kiss, and he was once tempted to make for his masterpiece, because Ireland breeds no poison, a deadly vapor in a Spaniard's fart — a deadly vapor that would have poisoned all Dublin."

Odors can kill, and one way to poison someone was to give them poisonous perfumed gloves. Smelling the perfume — which was deadly — poisoned the smeller.

Flamineo and Brachiano were joking, of course, about poisoning a Spaniard's fart, although a Spaniard named Don Diego famously farted in St. Paul's Cathedral in the late sixteenth century.

Brachiano said, "Oh, Saint Anthony's fire!"

Doctor Julio said to Brachiano, "Your secretary is merry, my lord."

So was Brachiano. Saint Anthony's fire is also known as *Ignis Sacer* or Holy Fire.

It is an acute infection that produces a fiery rash. Brachiano was using the phrase to refer to a fiery fart.

Flamineo said to Doctor Julio, "Oh, thou cursed antipathy to nature!"

He said to Brachiano, "Look, his eye's bloodshot, like a needle a surgeon stitches a wound with."

He then said to Doctor Julio, "Let me embrace thee, toad, and love thee, oh, thou abominable, loathsome gargle that will fetch up lungs, lights, heart, and liver, by very small quantities!"

In this society, "lights" was another word for lungs.

Brachiano said, "No more joking."

He then said to Doctor Julio, "I must employ thee, honest doctor. You must go to Padua, and by the way, use some of your skill for us."

"Sir, I shall," Doctor Julio said.

Brachiano asked, "But as for Camillo?"

Flamineo said, "He dies this night, by such an ingenious means that men shall suppose him slain by his own contrivance.

"But as for your duchess' death —"

Doctor Julio said, "I'll make sure she dies."

Brachiano said, "Small mischiefs are by greater made safe and secure."

Flamineo said to Doctor Julio, "Remember this, you slave. When knaves rise in society, they rise as gallows in the Low Countries, one upon another's shoulders."

In the Netherlands, when necessary, a prisoner could support another prisoner (who had a noose around his neck) on his shoulders and then step away and leave the other prisoner hanging until dead.

Brachiano, Flamineo, and Doctor Julio exited.

All this time, Cardinal Monticelso, Camillo, and Francisco de Medici had been talking to each other.

Cardinal Monticelso gave Camillo a piece of paper and said, "Here is an emblem, nephew; please look at it. It was thrown in at your window."

"At my window!" Camillo said.

He then looked at the emblem, which was a drawing with a motto. The emblem expressed a moral fable or allegory.

Camillo described the emblem: "Here is a stag, my lord, that has shed his horns, and, for the loss of them, the poor beast weeps. The motto is this: *Inopem me copia fecit*."

The Latin meant, "Abundance has made me poor."

The Latin came from Ovid's *Metamorphoses*, Book III, line 466. In the line, Narcissus complains to himself. He is so beautiful that he has fallen in love with his reflection in a pool of water. He has an abundance of love, but he loves so strongly that he cannot leave his reflection. Eventually, he is metamorphosed into a gold and white flower.

Camillo had an abundance, too. His wife seemed to be abundantly sexual, but not with him. Everyone believed that she was having an affair with Brachiano.

Cardinal Monticelso interpreted the emblem: "That is, plenty of horns has made him poor of horns."

Being a cuckold made Camillo less masculine. Horns are a sign of masculinity in deer.

Camillo asked, "What does that mean?"

"I'll tell you," Cardinal Monticelso said. "It is widely reported that you are a cuckold: Your wife is unfaithful to you."

Camillo asked, "Is it so widely reported? I would prefer that such reports as that, my lord, would keep within doors."

Francisco de Medici asked, "Do you have any children?"

"None, my lord," Camillo said.

"You are the happier because you have no children," Francisco de Medici said. "I'll tell you a tale."

"Please do, my lord," Camillo said.

Francisco de Medici said, "This is an old tale.

"Once upon a time Phoebus, the god of light — or he whom we call the Sun, wanted to be married. The gods gave their consent, and Mercury the messenger god was sent to announce it to the general world.

"But what a piteous cry immediately arose among the blacksmiths and felt-makers, brewers and cooks, reapers and butter-women, and among fishmongers and a thousand other trades, the workers in which are annoyed by the Sun's excessive heat! It was lamentable.

"They came to Jupiter all in a sweat, and they forbid the marriage. A great fat cook was made their speaker, who begged Jove, the king of the gods, that Phoebus the Sun-god might be gelded so he would be unable to have children. For if now, when there was but one Sun, so many men seemed likely to perish by his violent heat, what would they do if he were married and would beget more Suns, and those children of his would make fireworks like their father?

"So say I, only I apply it to your wife. Her having children, if Providence does not prevent her from having children, would make both nature, time, and man repent it."

Cardinal Monticelso said, "Look, nephew, go, change the air for shame — move to a different location and see if your absence will blast your cornucopia."

A cornucopia is a horn of plenty. In Camillo's case, he had a plenty of horns. Cardinal Monticelso was saying that Camillo would lose his horns if he were to move to a new location.

If the emblem were correct, and Camillo were to lose his horns, perhaps by moving to a different location, he would regret it. Something bad would happen. A cornucopia is a horn of plenty of good things, and Camillo would lose those good things. The good things in life often include life.

Cardinal Monticelso added, "Marcello has been chosen to be joint commissioner with you. Your job is to relieve our Italian coast from pirates."

Marcello said, "I am much honored by it."

Marcello was an attendant of the Duke of Florence, and he was the brother to Flamineo and Vittoria. Marcello and Camillo were brothers-in-law.

Camillo said, "But, sir, before I return, the stag's horns may be sprouted even greater than those that are shed."

He might be able to get rid of the horns he had now, but he could acquire even bigger horns while he was away.

Cardinal Monticelso said, "Do not fear it; I'll be your ranger."

He would watch Vittoria the way a game-ranger watched his deer.

Camillo said, "You must watch in the nights; the night is when there is the most danger."

Francisco de Medici said, "Farewell, good Marcello. May you bring all the best fortunes of a soldier's wish with you on shipboard."

Camillo asked, "Wouldn't it be best, now that I am turned soldier, for me before I leave my wife, to sell all she has, and then take leave of her?"

Cardinal Monticelso said, "I expect good from you, your parting is so merry."

In other words: You must be joking.

Camillo said, "My merry lord!"

In other words: You must be joking.

Camillo, who had been made a sea captain so he could go after pirates, added, "As the captain's right mood, I am resolved to be drunk this night."

He felt that in his particular situation, getting drunk was the right thing to do.

Camillo and Marcello exited.

Francisco de Medici said, "So, that was well done; now we shall discern how Camillo's desired absence will give violent way to Duke Brachiano's lust."

Brachiano desired Camillo's absence. With Camillo absent, Brachiano could spend more time with Vittoria, Camillo's wife.

Cardinal Monticelso said, "Why, that was it. That was why we gave Camillo a reason to be absent. To what scorned purpose else should we make choice of him to be a sea captain? And, besides, Count Lodovico, who was rumored to be a pirate, is now in Padua."

Francisco de Medici asked, "Is that true?"

Cardinal Monticelso replied, "Most certainly. I have letters from him, letters that supplicate me to work for his quick repeal from banishment. He means to address himself for pension to our sister duchess."

A pension is a periodic payment of money.

The Duchess of Brachiano was Francisco de Medici's sister but not Cardinal Monticelso's. Cardinal Monticelso was using "sister" as a courtesy title.

Francisco de Medici said, "Oh, that is well! We shall not want Camillo's absence past six days. I would happily have the Duke Brachiano run into notorious scandal; for there's nothing in such cursed dotage to repair his name, except the deep sense of some deathless shame."

One way to reform Brachiano would be to cause him severe embarrassment.

Cardinal Monticelso said, "It may be objected that I am dishonorable to play with and treat like this my kinsman: my nephew, Camillo. But I answer that for my revenge I'd stake a brother's life — the life of a brother who was wronged but dared not avenge himself."

Francisco de Medici said, "Come, let's see this strumpet."

Cardinal Monticelso said, "This is the curse of greatness!"

The curse of greatness is feeling that one is better than other people, and so if one desires someone else's wife, one can take her. Power corrupts, and absolute power corrupts absolutely.

Cardinal Monticelso asked, "Surely he'll not leave her?"

Surely Brachiano wouldn't leave Vittoria, although other people would like him to leave her.

Francisco de Medici said, "There's small cause of pity in him not leaving her."

They felt little pity for Camillo.

As for Brachiano and Vittoria, Francisco de Medici said:

"Like mistletoe on sere, dry, withered elms spent by weather,

"Let him cleave to her, and let both rot together."

Brachiano talked to a conjurer.

Brachiano said, "Now, sir, I claim your promise. It is dead midnight, the time set by you to show me by your art how the intended murder of Camillo and our loathed duchess grow to action."

The conjuror had promised to let him see their murders.

The conjurer replied, "You have won me by your bounty to a deed I do not often practice. Some there are who use sophistic tricks as they aspire to acquire that name which I would gladly lose: the name of necromancer. Some are accustomed to 'practice' the occult arts with cards, but they only seem to conjure, when indeed they are cheating. Others raise up their confederate spirits about windmills, and endanger their own necks for the making of a squib."

Windmills are figuratively fanciful projects; think of Don Quixote tilting at windmills. Squibs are small explosive devices.

The conjurer continued, "And some there are who will keep a gelding to show juggling tricks, and give out it is a spirit."

A man named Mr. Banks travelled with a performing horse named Morocco who could do such tricks as reacting positively to hearing the name of Queen Elizabeth and negatively to hearing the name of the King of Spain. Mr. Banks, however, apparently did not say that his horse was a spirit: Doing so could have gotten him killed for practicing witchcraft.

The conjurer continued, "Besides these, such a whole realm and ream of almanac-makers, figure-flingers, fellows, indeed, who live only by stealth, since they are merely lying about stolen goods — they'd make men think the devil were fast and loose, with speaking fustian Latin."

The conjuror was capable of wit. The almanac-makers used quite a lot of paper, and so the phrase "ream of almanac-makers" was an apt use of words.

An astrologer — a figure-flinger — could claim to be able to cast a horoscope to find out the location of stolen goods and to identify the thief.

The conjuror continued, "Please, sit down. Put on this nightcap, sir — it is charmed. And now I'll show you, by my strong and commanding art, the circumstance that breaks your duchess' heart."

A dumb show — a show in which the characters do not speak — appeared before them. Music played during it.

Acting in a suspicious manner, Doctor Julio and a man named Christophero entered the bedchamber of Isabella, Brachiano's wife. Doctor Julio and Christophero drew back a curtain behind which Brachiano's portrait was located — the curtain was intended to protect the portrait.

Doctor Julio and Christophero put on protective glass spectacles that covered their eyes and noses, and then they burned perfumes in front of the portrait, and they smeared a liquid substance on the lips of the portrait. Once that was done, they quenched the fire, took off their spectacles, and departed, laughing.

Isabella, wearing her nightgown, entered her bedchamber, ready to go to bed. She and others were carrying candles. Following her were Count Lodovico, young Giovanni, a man named Guidantonio, and others waiting on and serving her. She knelt down to pray, and then she drew back the curtain of the portrait, curtsied three times to it, and kissed it three times. She fainted, recovered slightly, and would not allow the others to come near the portrait, and then she died. Young Giovanni and Count Lodovico expressed their sorrow. Isabella was then conveyed out solemnly.

"Excellent!" Brachiano said. "So then she's dead."

"She's poisoned by the perfumed portrait," the conjuror said. "It was her nightly custom, before she went to bed, to go and visit your portrait, and to feed her eyes and lips on the lifeless image. Doctor Julio, observing this, infected it with perfumed oil and other poisoned stuff, which immediately suffocated her spirits."

Brachiano said, "I thought I saw Count Lodovico there."

'He was there," the conjuror said, "and by my art I find he did most passionately dote upon your duchess. Now turn another way, and view Camillo's far more cunningly contrived fate.

"Strike louder, music, from this charmed ground, to yield, as is appropriate for the act, a tragic sound!"

A second dumb show appeared. Music played during it.

Flamineo, Marcello, Camillo, and four more captains appeared. They drank healths, and they danced. A vaulting horse was brought into the room. Some men whispered to Marcello and two other men, and the three men went out of the room, while Flamineo and Camillo stripped off some of their clothing in preparation for vaulting. They complimented each other while deciding who would vault first. As Camillo was about to vault, Flamineo threw him on the floor upon his neck, and, with the help of the other men present — Marcello and two other men were still absent — writhed his neck about. Flamineo checked to make sure that Camillo's neck was broken and then lay him folded double under the vaulting horse. He then made a show of calling for help. Marcello came in, lamented, and sent for Cardinal Monticelso and the Duke of Florence (Francisco de Medici), who came forth with armed men. They wondered at the act, commanded that Camillo's body be carried home, and arrested Flamineo, Marcello, and the rest. They then went off to arrest Vittoria.

Brachiano said, "It was skillfully done; but yet I don't fully understand each thing that happened."

The conjurer said, "Oh, it was very apparent! You saw them enter, drink with their deep draughts to their prosperous voyage; and, to second that, Flamineo called to have a vaulting horse so they could continue their entertainment. The virtuous Marcello, who is innocent, was drawn from the room by use of a plot. Your eyes saw the rest, and they can inform you about the contrivance of it all."

Brachiano said, "It seems that Marcello and Flamineo have both been arrested."

The conjurer said, "Yes, you saw them guarded, and now people have come with the purpose of arresting your mistress, fair Vittoria. We are now beneath her roof. It would be a good idea for us to immediately leave by some back door."

Brachiano said, "Noble friend, you bind me forever to you. This handshake shall stand as the firm seal attached to my signature. It shall ensure that I pay you."

The conjurer said, "Sir, I thank you."

Brachiano exited.

The conjurer said:

"Both flowers and weeds spring, when the sun is warm,

"And great men do great good, or else great harm."

CHAPTER 3

— 3.1 —

Francisco de Medici and Cardinal Monticelso talked together. Their Chancellor and Registrar were present. They were in an anteroom to the courtroom where Vittoria's trial would take place.

Francisco de Medici said to Cardinal Monticelso, "You have dealt discreetly to obtain the presence of all the great lieger — resident — ambassadors to hear Vittoria's trial."

Cardinal Monticelso said, "It was not ill to have done so. For, sir, you know we have nothing but circumstantial evidence to charge her with about her husband's death. Their attestation of the truth, therefore, of the pieces of evidence of her black lust shall make her infamous to all our neighboring kingdoms."

He paused and then asked, "I wonder if Brachiano will be here?"

Francisco de Medici said, "Oh, bah! That impudence would be too palpable."

They exited.

Flamineo and Marcello entered, accompanied by guards and a lawyer.

The lawyer asked, "What, are you in by the week?"

In other words: Have you been caught?

The lawyer continued, "So — I will try now whether thy wit be close prisoner — I think no one should sit upon thy sister, except old whore-masters —"

"Sit upon" meant "sit in judgment upon."

Flamineo and Marcello were brothers, and Vittoria was their sister.

Flamineo interrupted, "Or cuckolds, for your cuckold is your most terrible tickler of lechery. Whoremasters would serve; for none are judges at tilting, except those who have been old tilters."

A "tickler" is 1) a chastiser, or 2) an exciter — perhaps a sexual exciter.

Tilting can be done with weapons, or with penises.

The lawyer said, "My lord Duke Brachiano and she have been very private."

He meant that they had done private things.

Flamineo said, "You are a dull ass; it is threatened that they have been very public."

He meant that what they had done or were suspected of doing was well known.

The lawyer said, "If it can be proved they have just kissed one another —"

"What then?" Flamineo asked.

The lawyer said, "My lord Cardinal Monticelso will ferret them."

To "ferret" meant to hunt. Figuratively, it meant to ask searching questions and hunt for a conviction.

Flamineo replied, "A cardinal, I hope, will not catch conies."

A cardinal is a bird, but not one of the kinds of birds that catch coneys (rabbits).

A coney is also a woman, and Catholic cardinals ought not to catch this kind of coney.

The lawyer said, "For to sow kisses — pay attention to what I say — to sow kisses is to reap lechery; and, I am sure, a woman who will endure kissing is half won."

Flamineo said, "True, her upper part is won, by that rule; if you will win her nether part, too, you know what follows."

By that rule, more kissing, but kissing on a different part of her body.

Trumpets sounded.

The lawyer said, "Listen! The ambassadors have arrived and have alighted from horseback or carriage."

To himself, Flamineo said, "I am putting on this feigned garb of mirth only in order to fool those who suspect me."

His sister was on trial, and if found guilty, her punishment would be severe. Flamineo was actually guilty of the murder, and if found guilty, his punishment would be severe.

Marcello said, "Oh, my unfortunate sister!"

Marcello said to Flamineo, "I wish that my dagger-point had cleft her heart when she first saw Brachiano. It is said that you were made his means, and his stalking horse, to ruin my sister."

Hunters would hide behind a stalking-horse while hunting game.

Flamineo and Marcello were brothers, and Vittoria was their sister.

Flamineo said, "I am a kind of path to her and my own preferment."

Marcello replied, "You mean your ruin."

Flamineo said, "Ha! Thou are a soldier; follow the great Duke of Florence, and feed his victories, as witches do their serviceable spirits, even with thy prodigal blood."

Witches were supposed to feed with blood the spirits that served them.

Flamineo then asked, "What have thou got? Only, like the wealth of captains, a poor handful, which in thy palm thou bear as men hold water. As you seek to grip it securely, the frail reward steals through thy fingers."

"Sir!" a shocked Marcello said.

Flamineo said, "Thou scarcely has the maintenance necessary to keep thee in fresh chamois."

Leather shirts worn underneath armor were called chamois.

"Brother!" a shocked Marcello said.

Flamineo said, "Hear me out. And thus, when we have even poured ourselves into great fights, for their ambition, or idle spleen, how shall we find reward?

"Just as we seldom find the mistletoe, which is sacred to medicine, on the used-to-build oak, without a poisonous mandrake plant by it, so in our quest of gain, alas, the poorest of the lord's feigned dislikes attempts to strike at a limb, but it strikes at the heart! This is lamented doctrine."

This culture believed that good plants such as mistletoe are usually found near poisonous plants such as mandrakes.

A lord may pretend to be angry and give what seems like a slight punishment, but actually it is a grievous punishment because the person suffering it has lost the favor of the lord.

"Come, come," Marcello said.

Flamineo was cynical; Marcello was not.

Flamineo said, "When age shall turn thee as white as a blooming hawthorn —"

Marcello said, "I'll interrupt you. For love of virtue bear an honest heart, and stride over every politic respect of the kind that, where they most advance, they most infect."

In other words: Have an honest heart simply because you love virtue. Do not seek to advance yourself through unscrupulous means.

He continued, "If I were your father, as I am your brother, I would not be ambitious to leave you with a better patrimony than that."

Flamineo said, "I'll think about that patrimony you recommend."

The Savoy ambassador entered the room.

Flamineo said, "Here come the lord ambassadors."

The lieger — resident — ambassadors passed through the room as they walked into the courtroom.

The French ambassador passed through the anteroom.

The lawyer said, "Oh, my sprightly Frenchman! Do you know him? He's an admirable tilter."

Flamineo said, "I saw him at the last tilting. He looked like a pewter candlestick fashioned like a man in armor, holding a tilting staff in his hand, little bigger than a candle of one-twelfth of a pound."

Flamineo's words had a bawdy meaning. One kind of tilting is done with a penis, and the French Ambassador's tilting staff weighed a little over an ounce.

The lawyer said, "Oh, but he's an excellent horseman!"

Flamineo said, "He's a lame one in his lofty tricks; he sleeps on horseback like a poulterer."

The word "lame" sometimes meant "impotent." The French ambassador slept rather than "tilted"; he was like a seller of eggs and poultry sleeping on a horse's broad back while on the way to market.

The English and Spanish ambassadors passed through the anteroom.

The lawyer said, "Look, the Spaniard ambassador!"

Flamineo said, "He carries his face in his ruff, as I have seen a serving-man carry glasses in a cypress hatband, monstrously steady, for fear of breaking. He looks like the claw of a blackbird, first salted and then cooked over a candle."

Fashionable Spaniards of the time wore wide ruffs. A ruff is a frill worn around the neck. A ruff is also a candle or a candlestick.

The arraignment of Vittoria was starting in the courtroom.

She was being tried for adultery and the murder of her husband.

Francisco de Medici, Cardinal Monticelso, the six lieger ambassadors, Brachiano, Vittoria, Zanche (Vittoria's serving-woman), Flamineo, Marcello, the lawyer, and a guard were present.

Cardinal Monticelso said to Brachiano, "Don't insist on attending the trial, my lord; here there is no place assigned to you. This business, by order of his Holiness, is left to our examination."

Brachiano replied, "May it thrive with you."

He lay a rich garment on the floor for him to sit on during the trial.

Francisco de Medici said, "There's a chair for his Lordship."

Brachiano said, "Don't insist on your kindness: An unbidden guest should travel as Dutch women go to church — they carry their stools with them."

Cardinal Monticelso replied, "As you please, sir."

He said to Vittoria, "Stand before the table, gentlewoman."

He then said to the lawyer prosecuting the case against Vittoria, "Now, signior, fall to your plea."

As was the legal custom, the lawyer spoke Latin: "*Domine judex, converte oculos in hanc pestem, mulierum corruptissiman.*"

["Lord Judge, look upon this plague, the most corrupt of women."]

Vittoria asked, "Who's he?"

Francisco de Medici replied, "A lawyer who pleads against you."

Vittoria said, "Please, my lord, let him speak his usual language: English. If he doesn't use English, I'll make no answer to what he says."

Francisco de Medici said, "Why, you understand Latin."

Vittoria replied, "I do, sir, but among these listeners who have come to hear my case, half or more may be ignorant of Latin."

Cardinal Monticelso said to the lawyer, "Go on, sir."

Vittoria said, "If you don't mind, I will not have my accusation clouded in a strange language: All this assembly shall hear — and understand — what you can charge me with."

Francisco de Medici said to the lawyer, "Signior, you need not much insist on using Latin; please, change your language."

Cardinal Monticelso said, "Oh, for God's sake!"

He then said to Vittoria, "Gentlewoman, your reputation shall be more famous if you insist on the prosecution using English."

He meant that if all the people in the courtroom understood the charges against her, they would spread the charges in their gossip, and her reputation would be widely known. Of course, the charges would give her a bad — an infamous — reputation.

The lawyer said to Vittoria, "Well, then, have at you."

"Have at you" were words used before beginning a fight. Think: *En garde*. Think: Prepare to be attacked.

Vittoria replied, "I am at the mark, sir; I'll give aim to you, and tell you how near you shoot."

She was using an archery metaphor. The mark was the target. She was standing by the target and would let him know how his shots fared: She would tell him if they hit the target, were close, or were wide of the mark.

The lawyer began to plead his case: "Most literated judges, may it please your lordships so to connive your judgments to the view of this debauched and diversivolent woman."

The lawyer used inflated language, and he sometimes misused words — a common result of trying to use inflated language.

"Literated" judges were literate judges.

The word "connive" means to shut one's eyes and ignore something that one dislikes. The lawyer was saying that the judges should shut their eyes to what they disliked about the woman, which would be what she was accused of doing. Of course, this was the opposite of what the lawyer wanted to happen: He wanted the judges to be fully aware of Vittoria's supposed bad points.

"Diversivolent" was a word of the lawyer's own making and perhaps meant "desiring strife" or "desiring differences." *Volo* is Latin for "I wish." The Latin *diverse* means "in different directions."

The lawyer continued, "Such a black concatenation of evil has effected this woman, and this woman has affected such a black concatenation of evil, that to extirp the memory of it, must be the consummation of her, and her projections —"

In other words: Such a black concatenation of evil had effected — created — Vittoria, and Vittoria had desired such a black concatenation of evil that to root up the memory of it, must be the consummation of her, and her projects —

"Consummation" means "the act of making perfect." The lawyer may have thought it meant "the act of consuming," as in being consumed by fire.

Vittoria interrupted, "What's all this?"

The lawyer said, "Hold your peace! Shut up! Exorbitant sins must have exulceration."

"Exulceration" means "ulceration," which is soreness.

Vittoria said, "Surely, my lords, this lawyer here has swallowed some apothecaries' bills, or proclamations, and now the hard and indigestible words come up, like stones we give to hawks for medicine. Why, this is Welsh to Latin."

Apothecaries' bills were medical prescriptions that were written in hard-to-understand jargon. Previously, Vittoria had worried that people attending the trial would not understand the lawyer's Latin, but the lawyer's inflated English was even harder to understand — it was like Welsh.

The lawyer said to the judges, "My lords, the woman does not know her tropes, nor her figures, nor does she perfectly understand the academic derivation of grammatical elocution."

In other words: Vittoria does not understand the use of rhetorical devices and figures of speech and the art of public speaking.

Francisco de Medici said, "Sir, your pains shall be well spared, and your deep eloquence shall be worthily applauded among those who understand you."

This was a small group, at best, and better described as those who pretend to understand you.

He was dismissing the lawyer.

The lawyer started to object, "My good lord —"

Francisco de Medici scornfully interrupted, "Sir, put up your papers in your fustian bag —"

He was punning. "Fustian" is 1) a kind of durable cloth, or 2) pompous speech.

He then said, "I ask your pardon, sir, your lawyer's bag is made of buckram, and I ask you to accept my notion of your learned verbosity."

Lawyer's bags were commonly made of the material called buckram.

The lawyer said, "I most graduatically thank your lordship: I shall have use for my pains elsewhere."

"Graduatically" meant "like a graduate."

The lawyer exited.

Cardinal Monticelso said to Vittoria, "I shall be plainer with you, and paint out your follies in more natural red and white than that upon your cheek."

He meant that he would talk more plainly than the lawyer had. He was also saying that Vittoria was wearing paint — cosmetics.

Vittoria said, "Oh, you are mistaken! You raise a blood as noble in this cheek as ever was your mother's."

In other words: You, Cardinal Monticelso, make me angry, and so my face becomes as red as ever was your mother's.

Cardinal Monticelso replied, "I must spare you for what you just said and not punish you until the evidence cries 'whore' to you."

Speaking as the prosecutor, Cardinal Monticelso said to the judges, "Observe this creature here, my honored lords, a woman of most prodigious spirit in her effected."

He was punning. One meaning of the sentence was that Vittoria was a woman of great courage — courage that had been produced in her.

But the word "spirit" could also mean semen, and the word "effected" could also mean ejaculated.

Vittoria said, "My honorable lord, it does not suit a reverend cardinal to play the lawyer thus."

Cardinal Monticelso said to her, "Oh, your trade instructs your language!"

He then said to the judges, "You see, my lords, what goodly fruit she seems to be. Yet like those apples that travellers report to be growing where Sodom and Gomorrah stood, I will only touch her, and you immediately shall see she'll fall to soot and ashes."

Deuteronomy 32:32 states, *"For their vine is of the vine of Sodom, and of the fields of Gomorrah: their grapes are grapes of gall, their clusters are bitter"* (King James Version).

Sir John Mandeville wrote this in his *Travels*:

"By the side of this sea grow trees that bear apples fine of color and delightful to look at; but when they are broken or cut, only ashes and dust and cinders are found

inside, as a token of the vengeance that God took on those five cities [including Sodom and Gomorrah] and the countryside round about, burning them with the fires of Hell."

Vittoria said, "Your envenomed apothecary should do it."

In other words: Your venomous apothecary should be able to poison me and turn my insides to soot and ashes.

Cardinal Monticelso said, "I am positive that if there were a second paradise to lose, this devil would betray it."

He was calling Vittoria a second Eve.

Vittoria said, "Oh, poor Charity! Thou are seldom found in scarlet."

Cardinals wore scarlet; so did lawyers.

Cardinal Monticelso said, "Who doesn't know that, when often night by night her gates were choked with coaches, and her rooms outbraved the stars with several kinds of lights, when she did counterfeit a prince's court in music, banquets, and most riotous surfeits, this whore indeed was 'hole-y'?"

Vittoria said, "Ha! Whore! What's that?"

Cardinal Monticelso said, "Shall I expound 'whore' to you? Surely I shall. I'll describe the character of whores perfectly.

"They are first, sweetmeats that rot the eater."

Whores give men venereal diseases.

He continued, "In man's nostrils they are poisoned perfumes.

"They are cozening alchemy, and shipwrecks in calmest weather."

Many alchemists were swindlers, although some were honest seekers after scientific knowledge. In Ben Jonson's *The Alchemist*, swindlers persuade a sucker to invest vast sums of money in an attempt to create a philosopher's stone that would turn base metals such as lead and iron into valuable metals such as silver and gold.

Cardinal Monticelso continued:

"What are whores!

"They are cold Russian winters, which appear so barren that it is as if nature had forgotten the spring.

"They are the true material fire of hell.

"They are worse than those tributes in the Low Countries — the Netherlands — paid, exactions upon meat, drink, garments, sleep, and aye, even on man's perdition, his sin."

Taxes on some products in the Netherlands sometimes equaled or exceeded the value of the product being purchased.

The cause of man's perdition, according to what Cardinal Monticelso was saying, is prostitution. Also according to the cardinal, in the Netherlands even prostitution was taxed.

Cardinal Monticelso continued, "Whores are those brittle evidences of law, which forfeit all a wretched man's estate for leaving out one syllable."

Sir Walter Raleigh lost his Sherbourne estate because of clerical errors.

Cardinal Monticelso continued:

"What are whores!

"They are those flattering bells that all have one tune at weddings and at funerals.

"Your rich whores are only treasuries filled by extortion, and emptied by cursed riot.

"They are worse, worse than dead bodies that are begged at gallows, and wrought upon by surgeons, to teach man in what respect he is imperfect."

Surgeons could beg for the corpses of hanged criminals so that they could dissect them and learn about the human body.

Cardinal Monticelso continued:

"What's a whore!

"She's like the guilty counterfeited coin, which, whoever first stamps it, brings into trouble all who receive it."

Vittoria said, "This character escapes me. I don't understand it."

Cardinal Monticelso said, "This character is you, gentlewoman!

"Take from all beasts and from all minerals their deadly poison —"

Vittoria interrupted, "Well, what then?"

Cardinal Monticelso said, "I'll tell thee. I'll find in thee an apothecary's shop, to sample them all."

According to Cardinal Monticelso, every poison can be found in the body of a whore.

The French ambassador said, "She has lived ill — she has behaved badly."

The English ambassador said, "True, but the cardinal's too bitter."

Cardinal Monticelso said, "You know what a whore is. After the devil Adultery, enters the devil Murder."

He believed that Vittoria was guilty of adultery (being a whore) and of murder.

Francisco de Medici said to Vittoria, "Your unhappy husband is dead."

Vittoria said, "Oh, he's a happy husband! Now he owes nature nothing."

Each of us owes a debt to nature. That debt is our death. (In this society, "debt" was pronounced much like "death.")

Francisco de Medici said, "And he died by a vaulting horse."

Cardinal Monticelso said, "It was an active plot; he jumped into his grave."

Francisco de Medici said, "What a prodigy was it, that from some two yards' height, a slender man should break his neck!"

Cardinal Monticelso said, "In the rushes!"

In this society, rushes were strewn on the floor as a kind of floor covering.

Francisco de Medici said, "And what's more, upon the instant he lost all use of speech and all vital motion, like a man who had lain in a winding sheet — a shroud — three days. Now note each circumstance of his death."

Cardinal Monticelso said, "And look upon this creature who was his wife! She comes not like a widow; she comes armed with scorn and impudence. Is this mourning-clothing you are wearing?"

It was not.

Vittoria said, "If I had foreknown that my husband would die, as you suggest, I would have ordered my mourning clothing."

"Oh, you are cunning!" Cardinal Monticelso said.

Vittoria replied, "You shame your wit and judgment to call it so. What! Is my just defense called impudence by him who is my judge? Let me appeal then from this Christian court to the uncivilized Tartar."

She believed that she was not receiving a fair trial.

Cardinal Monticelso said, "See, my lords. She defames our proceedings."

Vittoria knelt and said, "Humbly thus, thus low to the most worthy and respected lieger ambassadors, my modesty and womanhood I tender; but, in addition, so entangled in a cursed accusation, that my defense, of necessity, like Perseus has done, must emblematically represent masculine virtue.

"Let me get to the point: If you find me guilty, then sever my head from my body, and we'll part good friends."

She stood up, looked at Cardinal Monticelso, and said, "I scorn to hold my life at yours, or any man's entreaty, sir."

The English ambassador said, "She has a brave spirit."

"Well, well," Cardinal Monticelso said, "such counterfeit jewels make true ones often suspected."

"You are deceived," Vittoria replied.

She said to the judges, "For know that all your strict, combined heads, which strike against this mine of diamonds, shall prove to be only glass hammers. They shall break. These are but feigned shadows of my 'evils.'"

The heads were 1) hammerheads, and 2) armies.

Vittoria continued, "Terrify babes, my lord, with painted devils: I am past such needless palsy — such needless shivering with fear.

"As for your names of 'whore' and 'murderess,' they proceed from you, as if a man should spit against the wind — the filth returns in his face."

Cardinal Monticelso said, "I ask you, mistress, to answer for me one question: Who lodged beneath your roof that deadly night your husband broke his neck?"

Brachiano said, "That question forces me to break my silence. I was there."

Cardinal Monticelso asked, "What was your business there?"

Brachiano replied, "Why, I came to comfort her, and take some course of action for settling her estate because I heard that her husband was in debt to you, my lord."

Cardinal Monticelso said, "He was in debt to me."

Brachiano said, "And it was strangely feared that you would cheat her."

Cardinal Monticelso asked, "Who made you the overseer of the estate?"

Brachiano said, "Why, my charity, my charity, which should flow from every generous and noble spirit to orphans and to widows."

Cardinal Monticelso said, "Your lust!"

Brachiano said, "Cowardly dogs bark loudest. Sirrah priest, I'll talk with you hereafter. Do you hear?"

His calling the cardinal "sirrah" was an insult.

Brachiano continued, "The sword you frame of such an excellent temper, I'll sheath in your own bowels."

The sword was the sword of justice, although Brachiano would probably call it a sword of injustice when it was in Cardinal Monticelso's hands.

The word "temper" referred to the cardinal's state of mind and the sword's state of hardness and elasticity.

Brachiano continued, "There are a number of thy coat who resemble your common post-boys."

His use of the word "thy" to apply to the cardinal was insulting.

"Post-boys" are letter carriers who ride horses.

Cardinal Monticelso snorted, "Ha!"

Brachiano replied, "Your mercenary post-boys. Your letters carry truth, but it is your practice to fill your mouths with gross and impudent lies."

He started to leave, leaving behind the garment on which he had been sitting.

A servant said, "My lord, your gown."

The gown was a loose upper garment that men wore.

Brachiano replied, "Thou lie — it was my stool. Bestow it upon thy master, who will claim the rest of the household-stuff, for Brachiano was never so beggarly to take a stool out of another's lodging. Let thy master make a valance for his bed out of it, or a demi-footcloth for his most reverend moil."

A demi-footcloth is a half-length cloth placed on a horse or mule to help protect its rider from mud and dust.

A moil is a hornless cow. Cardinals customarily rode on mules.

The word "moil" can also mean "tumult" or "drudgery" or "mud and mire."

Brachiano continued, "Monticelso, *nemo me impune lacessit.*"

["Monticelso, no one provokes me with impunity."]

He exited.

Cardinal Monticelso said, "Your champion's gone."

Vittoria replied, "The wolf may prey the better."

Chances are, she was punning on "pray."

Francisco de Medici said, "My lord, there's great suspicion about the murder, but no sound proof who did it. For my part, I do not think she has a soul so black to do a deed so bloody; if she has, as in cold countries husbandmen plant vines, and with warm blood manure them, then even so one summer she will bear unsavory fruit, and before next spring wither both branch and root."

Blood meal is powdered dried animal blood; it was used as a fertilizer to boost the nitrogen level in soil.

He continued, "Let pass the act of blood and only descend to matters of incontinence."

He was advocating that Vittoria not be tried for the crime of murder — just for adultery. Incontinence is being unable to control oneself; in the case of adultery, it is being unable to control one's lust.

Vittoria said, "I discern poison under your gilded pills."

Imagine a poisoned pill covered with gold foil. Its appearance is much different from its reality. Vittoria knew that Francisco de Medici was not her friend. If anything, he was playing good cop to the cardinal's bad cop.

Cardinal Monticelso said, "Now that the Duke of Brachiano's gone, I will produce a letter wherein it was plotted that he and you should meet at an apothecary's summer-house, down by the River Tiber."

He produced the letter and gave it to the judges, saying, "View it, my lords, where after wanton bathing and the heat of a lascivious banquet — please read it, I am ashamed to speak out loud the contents of the rest of the letter."

Vittoria said, "Grant that I was tempted, but temptation to lust does not prove that the act of lust was committed: *Casta est quam nemo rogavit.*"

The Latin words meant, "She is chaste whom no man has asked." They were from Ovid's *Amores* I.viii.43.

This seems an odd quotation to say because the letter would seem to be an invitation to commit adultery in the summer-house.

Vittoria, however, continued, "You read his hot love to me, but you lack my frosty answer to him."

Her point may have been that no one was asking her for her testimony and evidence. The trial had a person to prosecute her, but it had no one to represent her and defend her — Cardinal Monticelso had waited until after Brachiano had exited to present this letter to the judges. If Vittoria were not given a fair trial and were not asked to give her testimony and present her evidence, then the assumption ought to be that she is chaste.

So far, many accusations had been made, but until this letter was produced, no real evidence had been presented — and the letter was at best circumstantial evidence: As Vittoria pointed out, it did not prove that she had committed adultery.

Cardinal Monticelso said, "Frost in the dog-days! Strange!"

The dog-days are the hottest days of summer in the Northern Hemisphere.

Vittoria said, "Do you condemn me because the Duke of Brachiano loved me? So may you blame some fair and crystal river because some melancholic, mentally disturbed man drowned himself in it."

She meant drowned in water.

Cardinal Monticelso said, "Truly drowned, indeed."

He meant drowned in lust.

Vittoria said, "Sum up my faults, I ask you, and you shall find that beauty and gay clothes, a merry heart, and a good appetite to feast, are all, all the poor crimes that you can charge me with. Truly, my lord, you might go shoot flies — the sport would be nobler."

"Very good," Cardinal Monticelso said sarcastically.

Vittoria said, "But take your course. It seems you've beggared me first, and now are eager to ruin me. I have houses, jewels, and a poor remnant of gold and silver Portuguese crusadoes — coins decorated with a cross.

"I wish those would make you charitable!"

Cardinal Monticelso said, "If the devil did ever take good shape, behold his picture."

He was saying that she was the image of the devil.

Of course, this was not a compliment, as Vittoria now acknowledged: "You have one virtue left, and that is that you will not flatter me."

Francisco de Medici asked, "Who brought you this letter?"

Vittoria replied, "I am not compelled to tell you."

Cardinal Monticelso said, "My lord Duke of Brachiano sent to you a thousand ducats on the twelfth of August."

Vittoria replied, "It was to keep your nephew — my husband — from being imprisoned; I paid interest for it."

Cardinal Monticelso said, "I rather think that it was interest for his lust."

"Who says so but yourself?" Vittoria said. "If you are my accuser, please cease to be my judge. Come away from the bench. Give your evidence against me, and let these lieger ambassadors be the moderators."

Certainly, Cardinal Monticelso was a biased judge. He had already made up his mind that she was guilty.

Vittoria continued, "My lord cardinal, if your intelligencing — spying — ears were so long as to reach to my thoughts, if you had an honest tongue, I would not care even if you proclaimed out loud all my thoughts."

Cardinal Monticelso said, "Bah! Bah! After your goodly and vainglorious banquet, I'll give you a choke-pear."

A choke-pear is a bitter, difficult-to-swallow fruit.

Vittoria asked, "Of your own grafting?"

In slang, because of its shape, a pear is a penis plus a scrotum. In grafting a branch to a different plant, a shoot is inserted into a slit so that sap can travel from one to the other. You can guess what the shoot, slit, and sap represent.

Cardinal Monticelso said, "You were born in Venice, honorably descended from the Vittelli family. It was my nephew's fate, ill may I name the hour, to marry you. He bought you from your father."

"Ha!" Vittoria said scornfully.

Cardinal Monticelso said, "He spent twelve thousand ducats there in six months, and (to my knowledge) received in dowry with you not one julio."

A julio was a coin struck by Pope Julius II.

Cardinal Monticelso continued, "It was a hard pennyworth, the ware being so light."

The word "light" can mean promiscuous.

He continued, "I so far have only drawn back the curtain; now I go on to your picture: You came from thence a most notorious strumpet, and so you have continued."

Vittoria said, "My lord!"

Cardinal Monticelso said, "Nay, hear me, you shall have time to prate. My Lord Brachiano — alas! I am only repeating what is ordinary gossip at the Rialto, a meeting place, and related in ballads, and would be played on the stage, except that vice many times finds such loud friends that preachers are charmed silent."

Plays about sin often appear on the theatrical stage, but the friends of this particular vice — adultery — charm preachers and make them silent. Because of that, the preachers don't preach against that sin on the stage that is their pulpit.

Cardinal Monticelso continued, "You, gentlemen — Flamineo and Marcello — the court has nothing now to charge you with, only you must remain upon your sureties for your appearance."

Flamineo and Marcello needed sureties — people who would ensure that they would appear in court when ordered.

Francisco de Medici said, "I stand as surety for Marcello."

Flamineo said, "And my lord Duke Brachiano stands as surety for me."

Cardinal Monticelso said, "As for you, Vittoria, your public — widely known — fault, joined to the condition of the present time, takes from you all the fruits of noble pity, such a corrupted trial you have made both of your life and beauty, and been styled no less an ominous fate than blazing stars to princes."

A fault can mean a crime or a sin.

Blazing stars — comets — were ominous signs for the great men and great women of the world.

Cardinal Monticelso continued, "Hear your sentence: You are confined to a house of convertites. And your bawd —"

Flamineo thought, *Who, I? Is he talking about me?*

Cardinal Monticelso continued, "— the Moor —"

Zanche, Vittoria's woman-servant, was a Moor. Zanche would accompany Vittoria as she served her sentence.

Flamineo thought, *Oh, I am a sound man again.*

Vittoria interrupted, "A house of convertites! What's that?"

Cardinal Monticelso answered, "A house of penitent whores."

Vittoria asked, "Do the noblemen in Rome erect it for their wives? Is that why I am sent to lodge there?"

"You must have patience," Francisco de Medici said.

"I must first have vengeance!" Vittoria replied. "I would like to know if you have your salvation by patent — by special decree — since you proceed this way."

Vittoria was saying that rather than getting salvation through sincere repentance, Cardinal Monticelso and Francisco de Medici must have gotten their salvation through politics.

Cardinal Monticelso said, "Away with her. Take her away from here."

Vittoria cried, "A rape! A rape!"

Cardinal Monticelso said, "What!"

Vittoria replied, "Yes, you have ravished — raped — justice and forced her to do your pleasure."

Cardinal Monticelso said, "Bah, she's mad —"

Vittoria said, "Die with those pills in your most cursed maw — those pills that ought to bring you health!"

A maw is the mouth of a voracious animal. The pills were the sentences that the cardinal had handed out without consulting the lieger ambassadors.

Vittorio continued, "Or while you sit on the bench, let your own spittle choke you!"

Cardinal Monticelso said, "She's turned into a Fury."

Vittoria said, "I wish that the last day — the Day of Judgment — may so find you, and leave you the same devil you were before!

"Instruct me, some good blood-sucker, to speak treason. For since you cannot take my life on account of my deeds, take my life on account of my words.

"Oh, woman's poor revenge, which dwells only in the tongue!"

She would have preferred taking revenge at the end of a sword.

"I will not weep," Vittoria continued. "No, I scorn to call up one poor tear to fawn on your injustice. Bear me away from here and to this house of — what's your mitigating title?"

Cardinal Monticelso answered, "Of convertites."

Vittoria said, "It shall not be a house of convertites. My mind shall make it honester to me than the Pope's palace, and more peaceable than thy soul, though thou are a cardinal.

"Know this, and let it somewhat raise your spite,

"Through darkness diamonds spread their richest light."

Vittoria considered herself to be a diamond.

A guard led her and Zanche away.

Brachiano entered the room and said to Francisco de Medici, "Now that you and I are friends, sir, we'll shake hands at a friend's grave together; it will be a fit place, being the emblem of soft peace, to atone our hatred."

Brachiano knew that Isabella, who was his wife and Francisco de Medici's sister, was dead.

"Sir, what's the matter?" Francisco de Medici asked.

Brachiano did not answer the question, but he said, "I will not chase more blood from that loved cheek. You have lost too much already; fare you well."

He exited.

Francisco de Medici said to himself, "How strange these words of his sound! What's the interpretation?"

Flamineo, who had overheard his master's words, said to himself, "Good! This is a preface to the discovery of the duchess' death. He carries it well. Because now I cannot counterfeit a whining passion for the death of my lady, I will feign a mad humor because of the disgrace of my sister, and that will keep off idle questions. Treason's tongue has a villainous palsy in it; I will talk to any man, hear no man, and for a time appear a politic madman."

By pretending to have become mentally disturbed because of the disgrace of his sister, Flamineo would keep people from asking him questions he didn't want to answer. He would be a politic madman — a "madman" with a cunning reason to be mad.

To Flamineo, it was easier to pretend to be insane than to pretend to feel sadness for Isabella's death.

Young Giovanni and Count Lodovico entered the room. Both had been present when Isabella, young Giovanni's mother, had died, as shown by the magic of the conjurer. Count Lodovico, according to the conjuror, had loved Isabella.

Francisco de Medici said, "How are you now, my noble nephew? What? Dressed in black!"

Young Giovanni replied, "Yes, uncle, I was taught to imitate you in virtue, and you must imitate me in the colors of your garments. My sweet mother is —"

Francisco de Medici asked, "How? Where?"

Young Giovanni said, "— is there."

Francisco de Medici looked around.

Young Giovanni said, "No, yonder. Indeed, sir, I'll not tell you, for I shall make you weep."

Francisco de Medici asked, "Is she dead?"

"Do not blame me now," young Giovanni said. "I did not tell you so."

"She's dead, my lord," Lodovico said.

"Dead!" Francisco de Medici said.

Cardinal Monticelso said, "Blessed lady, thou are now above thy woes!"

He asked the resident ambassadors, "Will it please your lordships to withdraw a little?"

The ambassadors withdrew.

Young Giovanni asked, "What do the dead do, uncle? Do they eat, hear music, go hunting, and be merry, as we who live do?"

Francisco de Medici said, "No, nephew; they sleep."

"Lord, Lord, I wish that I were dead!" young Giovanni said. "I have not slept these past six nights. When do they wake?"

"When God shall please," Francisco de Medici answered.

"Good God, let her sleep always," young Giovanni said, "for I have known her to stay awake a hundred nights, when all the pillow where she laid her head was salt-wet with her tears. I must complain to you, sir. I'll tell you how they have treated her now she's dead. They wrapped her in a cruel fold of lead, and they would not let me kiss her."

A fold is a wrapping or an embrace. A fold of lead is a kind of lead wrapping-sheet, aka shroud.

Francisco de Medici asked, "Did thou love her?"

Young Giovanni said, "I have often heard her say she gave me suck, and it would seem by that she dearly loved me, since princes seldom do it."

In this society, princes need not necessarily be male. Upper-class woman often did not suckle their own children; they used wet nurses instead to do that.

Francisco de Medici said, "Oh, all of my poor sister that remains!"

Isabella had only one child: young Giovanni.

Francisco de Medici ordered, "Take him away for God's sake!"

An attendant led young Giovanni away.

Cardinal Monticelso asked, "How are you now, my lord?"

Francisco de Medici answered, "Believe me, I am nothing but her grave, and I shall keep her blessed memory longer than a thousand epitaphs."

Flamineo was at one end of an antechamber to the courtroom. Marcello and Lodovico were at the other end.

Flamineo had started to pretend to be mentally disturbed because of the disgrace of his sister, Vittoria.

He said, "We endure the strokes like anvils or hard steel, until pain itself makes us no pain to feel.

"Who shall do me right and justice now?

"Is this the end — the purpose — of service?

"I'd rather go weed garlic, work my way through France, and be my own hostler.

"I'd rather wear sheepskin underwear or shoes that stink of blacking — polish — and be entered into the list of the forty thousand peddlers in Poland."

The Savoy ambassador entered the antechamber.

Flamineo continued, "I wish that I had rotted in some surgeon's house at Venice, built upon the pox as well as upon piles, before I had served Brachiano!'

The surgeon had made the money to build the house by treating the pox (syphilis) and piles (hemorrhoids).

The word "piles" was a pun; the word also meant the foundation that was especially necessary in a city such as Venice.

The Savoy ambassador said, "You must have comfort."

Flamineo replied, "Your comfortable words are like honey: They relish well in your mouth that's whole, but in my mouth that's wounded, they go down as if the sting of the bee were in them."

To a man who is ill, honey can taste bitter.

Flamineo continued, "Oh, they have wrought their purpose cunningly, as if they would not seem to do it out of malice! In this a politician imitates the devil, as the devil imitates a cannon: Wherever he comes to do mischief, he comes with his backside towards you."

Politicians (people who act craftily and deviously) and devils can do damage indirectly rather than through frontal assault.

Witches were believed to kiss the devil's bare buttocks as a sign of obedience.

The French ambassador entered the antechamber and said, "The proofs of Vittoria's guilt are evident."

Flamineo said, "Proof! It was corruption, not proof. Oh, gold, what a god are thou! And oh, man, what a devil are thou to be tempted by that cursed mineral! Your diversivolent lawyer, watch him closely!"

He was using the same word that the lawyer had used against Vittoria before being dismissed from the courtroom.

Flamineo continued, "Knaves turn informers, as maggots turn into flies — you may catch gudgeons with either."

Literally, "gudgeons" are small, easily caught fish. Figuratively, they are gullible simpletons.

Flamineo continued, "A cardinal! I wish he could hear me! There's nothing so holy but money will corrupt and putrify it, like food in the heat under the line of the equator."

The English ambassador entered the antechamber.

Flamineo said to him, "You are happy in England, my lord; here they sell justice with those weights they press men to death with. Oh, horrible reward!"

Men who refused to plead either innocent or guilty in trials had heavy weights placed on top of them until they either pleaded or died. Some people chose to die this way because they believed that they would be found guilty, and their estate would be forfeited, thereby leaving their family members destitute.

This law was followed in what became the United States. On 19 September 1692, Giles Corey died from being pressed after declining to plead in the Salem Witch Trials. Whenever he was asked to plead, he replied, "More weight."

The English Ambassador said, "Come on, Flamineo. Bah."

Flamineo replied, "Bells never ring well until they are at their full pitch, and I hope yonder cardinal shall never have the grace to pray well until he comes to the scaffold."

A full pitch comes from a full swing, and Flamineo was saying he wanted Cardinal Monticelso to swing at the end of a noose.

Pitch is the height that a falcon will climb before steeply swooping down with wings folded back.

The ambassadors exited.

Flamineo said, "If they — Cardinal Monticelso and Francisco de Medici — would be racked now to know the conspiracy! But your noblemen are privileged from being tortured on the rack — and it's a good thing — because a little thing would pull some of them to pieces before they came to their arraignment."

Some noblemen are already so metaphorically rotten that being stretched on the rack even a little would tear them to pieces.

Flamineo continued, "Religion, oh, how it is commeddled and commingled with policy! The first blood shed in the world happened about religion. I wish I were a Jew!"

The first murder occurred when Cain slew Abel. See Genesis 4.1-16.

Referring to Jews, Marcello said, "Oh, there are too many!"

Flamineo replied, "You are deceived; there are not Jews enough, priests enough, nor gentlemen enough."

Marcello asked, "What do you mean?"

Flamineo said, "I'll prove it. If there were Jews enough, so many Christians would not turn usurers."

In the Middle Ages and beyond, many Jews became usurers because of Biblical laws against lending at interest: Christians would not do that job.

Flamineo continued, "If there were priests enough, one priest would not have six benefices."

A benefice was an appointment that gave a priest an income. The more benefices, the more money, but the more benefices, the more likelihood that the priest could not do the job that he was supposed to be doing.

Flamineo continued, "And if there were gentlemen enough, then so many early mushrooms, whose best growth sprang from a dunghill, would not aspire to gentility."

A mushroom was figuratively an upstart: a man who rose rapidly to a good social standing.

Flamineo continued, "Farewell. Let others live by begging. Be thou one of them — practice the art of Wolner in England, to swallow all that is given to thee: and yet let one purgation make thee as hungry again as fellows who work in a sawpit.

"I'll go hear the screech-owl."

Wolner was a famous glutton who was thought to be able to eat iron, glass, and oyster shells.

The cry of the screech-owl was regarded as ominous.

Flamineo exited.

Lodovico, who had been listening to Flamineo, said, "This was Brachiano's pander; and it is strange that in such open and apparent guilt of his adulterous sister, he dares to express so scandalous a passion. I must sniff him out and discover his secrets."

Flamineo re-entered, saw Lodovico, and said to himself, "How dare this banished count return to Rome with his pardon not yet acquired! I have heard that the deceased duchess gave him a pension, and that he came along from Padua in the train of the young prince. There's something going on.

"Physicians, who cure poisons, still work with counter-poisons."

A counter-poison is an antidote, but Flamineo was thinking of one poison being used to counteract another poison. Swallowing a second poison can cause a person to vomit up the first poison (and the second).

Flamineo and Lodovico were both poisons — they were evil men. One kind of counter-poison would be hiring an evil man to do evil in order to punish the doer of an evil deed. Flamineo could guess that Lodovico was a counter-poison to punish him.

Marcello said to himself, "Pay attention to this strange encounter."

Flamineo and Lodovico began to talk together. Both men were more capable of feeling hostility than of feeling affection.

Flamineo continued to pretend to be mentally disturbed as the two men began to insult each other.

Flamineo said, "May the god of melancholy turn thy gall to poison, and similar to the boisterous waves in a rough tide, let one of the stigmatic — ugly and indicative of criminality — wrinkles in thy face always overtake another."

Lodovico replied, "I do thank thee, and I wish ingeniously and ingenuously, for thy sake, the dog-days all year long."

The dog-days were very hot days. They were good days to drink alcohol, which increased lustful desire. At such a time, panders could do well.

Flamineo asked, "How croaks the raven?"

The croak of the raven was regarded as ominous.

He then asked, "Is our good duchess dead?"

Lodovico replied, "Yes, she is dead."

Flamineo said, "Oh, fate! Misfortune comes like the coroner's business — huddle upon huddle, heap upon heap, pile upon pile."

Lodovico asked, "Shall thou and I join housekeeping and live in the same home?"

Flamineo replied, "Yes, I am content to do that."

If they were to live together, they needed to agree on some "rules."

What kind of rules would two murderers agree to?

Flamineo said, "Let's be unsociably sociable."

Lodovico said, "We shall sit some three days together, and talk."

Flamineo replied, "Only by making faces."

He added, "We will lie in our clothes."

Lodovico said, "With bundles of sticks for our pillows."

Flamineo said, "And we shall be louse-y."

Lice were a problem for human beings at this time.

Lodovico said, "In taffeta underwear — that's genteel melancholy. We will sleep all day."

Flamineo said, "Yes; and, like your melancholic hare, we will feed after midnight."

Antonelli and Gasparo, friends of Francisco de Medici, entered the antechamber. They were laughing; they had good news to give to Count Lodovico.

"We are observed," Flamineo said. "See how yonder couple 'grieves.'"

"What a strange creature is a laughing fool!" Lodovico said. "As if man were created for no purpose other than to show his teeth."

Flamineo said, "I'll tell thee what, it would do well instead of looking-glasses, to set one's face each morning by a saucer of a witch's congealed blood."

A saucer of a witch's congealed blood would make a poor mirror, but "to set one's face" meant to put on one's face a fixed facial expression. In this case, such a facial expression is unlikely to be kindly.

Lodovico said, "Precious girn, rogue!"

A girn is a snarl.

He added, "We'll never part."

In Dante's *Inferno*, various kinds of sinners are grouped together forever: The thieves are with the thieves, the flatterers are with the flatterers, etc.

Flamineo replied, "Never, until the beggary of courtiers, the discontent of churchmen, a lack of soldiers, and all the creatures who hang manacled, worse than strappadoed, on the lowest part of fortune's wheel, be taught, in our two lives, to scorn that world which deprives life of the means of livelihood."

Both Lodovico and Flamineo deprived men of life and therefore of the means of livelihood.

A man who is strappadoed is tortured by having his hands bound together behind his back and then being lifted into the air by those hands.

What would it take to make many people scorn a world that deprives life of the means of livelihood? Courtiers would have to become beggars, churchmen would have to become discontented, soldiers would have to be lacking (and so armies could not protect citizens), and many people would have to be tortured by being strappadoed. For people to scorn a world that deprives life of the means of livelihood, they would have to live that kind of life. Some people, of course, already live that kind of life — for example, those at the bottom of the wheel of fortune.

Antonelli came over to Count Lodovico and said, "My lord, I bring good news. The Pope, on his deathbed, at the earnest suit of the great Duke of Florence — Francisco de Medici — has signed your pardon, and restored unto you —"

Lodovico interrupted, "I thank you for your news. Look up again, Flamineo, and see my pardon."

Flamineo asked Lodovico, "Why do you laugh? There was no such condition in our contract."

Lodovico asked, "Why do I laugh?"

Flamineo was not making sense.

Flamineo said, "You shall not seem to be a happier man than I am. You know our vow, sir; if you will be merry, do it in the like posture, as if some great man sat while his enemy was being executed. Though it be just like enjoyable lechery to thee, do it with a crabbed politician's face."

Some politicians inwardly rejoice when an enemy is executed, but they maintain a dignified, sober expression during the execution.

Lodovico laughed and said, "Your sister is a damnable whore."

Flamineo said, "Ha!"

Lodovico said, "Notice that I spoke that while laughing."

Flamineo said, "Do thou think to ever speak again?"

Lodovico said, "Hear what I say now. Will thou sell me forty ounces of her blood so I can water a mandrake?"

If Vittoria were executed by being beheaded, she would bleed. Mandrakes were supposed to feed on blood, and they were supposed to grow near gallows.

Flamineo said, "Poor lord, you did vow to live as a louse-y creature."

"Yes," Lodovico said.

Flamineo said, "Like one who had forever forfeited the daylight, by being in debt."

A bankrupt could live out his life in prison and never again see the Sun. Prisons were infested with lice.

"Ha, ha!" Lodovico laughed.

Flamineo said, "I do not greatly wonder you do break: Your lordship learned how to do it long ago."

Flamineo was saying that Lodovico was breaking his word, and Flamineo was saying that Lodovico knew about going bankrupt.

"But I'll tell you," Flamineo continued.

"Tell me what?" Lodovico asked.

"And it shall stick by you," Flamineo said.

"I long for it," Lodovico said.

"This laughter scurvily becomes your face," Flamineo said. "If you will not be melancholy, be angry."

He hit Lodovico in the face, laughed, and said, "See, now I laugh, too."

Marcello said to Flamineo, his brother, "You are to blame, and you are too blameworthy. I'll force you away from here."

Lodovico drew his sword and lunged at Flamineo.

Antonelli and Gasparo restrained Lodovico.

Marcello restrained Flamineo.

Lodovico ordered, "Unhand me."

Marcello and Flamineo exited, and Antonelli and Gasparo released Lodovico.

Very angry, Lodovico said, "That I should ever be forced to right myself and vindicate my honor upon a pander!"

Antonelli said, "My lord."

Ignoring him, Lodovico said, "He had been as good met a thunderbolt with his fist."

Gasparo said, "How this shows!"

Lodovico's display of anger showed badly.

This society looked down upon excessive displays of anger. It valued controlling one's emotions.

Lodovico swore, "By God's death!"

He added, "How did my sword miss him? These rogues who are most weary of their lives always escape the greatest dangers. A pox upon him; all his reputation, nay, all the goodness of his family, is not worth half this earthquake. I learned from no fencer how to shake like this."

He was shaking with anger.

Fencers need to stay calm while fencing.

Lodovico said to Antonelli and Gasparo, "Come, I'll forget him, and go drink some wine."

CHAPTER 4

— 4.1 —

Francisco de Medici and Cardinal Monticelso talked together in a room in Francisco de Medici's palace in Rome.

Cardinal Monticelso said, "Come, come, my lord, untie your folded thoughts, and let them dangle loose, as a bride's hair."

In this society, virgin brides wore their hair loose.

He then said, "Your sister's poisoned."

Francisco de Medici replied, "Far be it from my thoughts to seek revenge."

Cardinal Monticelso asked, "Are you turned into all marble? Have you no feelings?"

Francisco de Medici replied, "Shall I defy the Duke of Brachiano and impose a war that will be very burdensome on my poor subjects' necks — a war I don't have the power to end at my will? You know, for all the murders, rapes, and thefts committed in the horrid lust of war, that man who unjustly caused the war to first proceed, shall find it in his grave, and in his seed."

A man who starts an unjust war shall be punished for it in the afterlife, and his descendants shall also be punished for his unjust actions.

Cardinal Monticelso said, "That's not the course of action I'd wish you to take; please pay attention to me. We see that undermining prevails more than do the cannon."

In warfare soldiers would create tunnels underneath the walls of castles or towns and use explosives to bring down the walls. Cardinal Monticelso was saying that being sneaky was more effective at getting revenge than a frontal attack such as using cannon to bring down a castle's or town's walls.

Cardinal Monticelso continued, "Bear your wrongs concealed, and, patient as the tortoise, let this camel stalk over your back without bruising it."

Camels had a reputation for being angry, while tortoises had a reputation for being subtle and crafty.

Cardinal Monticelso was advising Francisco de Medici to allow him to get Francisco's revenge against Brachiano.

He said, "Sleep with the lion, and let this brood of secure foolish mice play with your nostrils, until the time shall be ripe for the bloody audit, and the fatal grip."

Cardinal Monticelso would be the lion, and he would be in league with Francisco de Medici and wait until the appropriate time to get revenge against Brachiano.

Cardinal Monticelso continued, "Aim like a cunning fowler and close one eye, so that you the better may your game spy."

A fowler hunts fowl, and archers close one eye while aiming at the target. The cardinal's advice was for Francisco de Medici to close one eye to whatever Cardinal Monticelso would do.

Francisco de Medici said, "Free me, my innocence, from treacherous acts! I know there's thunder yonder; and I'll stand, like a safe valley, which low bends the knee to some aspiring mountain —"

If he was using "my innocence" to refer to "my Cardinal Monticelso," he was using the phrase ironically.

The thunder is the vengeance of God.

Could "some aspiring mountain" be Cardinal Monticelso?

Francisco de Medici continued, "— since I know that treason, like spiders weaving nets for flies, by her foul work is found, and in her foul work treason dies."

Making war against a powerful man such as a duke could be regarded as a kind of treason.

He continued, "To pass away these thoughts, my honored lord, it is reported you possess a book wherein you have recorded, using secret intelligence gathered by informers and spies, the names of all notorious offenders and criminals lurking about the city."

"Sir, I do," Cardinal Monticelso replied. "And some there are who call it my black-book."

A black-book is a book of black magic.

He continued, "Well may the title hold; for although it doesn't teach the art of conjuring, yet in it lurk the names of many devils."

Francisco de Medici said, "Please let me see it."

"I'll fetch it to your lordship," Cardinal Monticelso said.

He exited to get the book.

Francisco de Medici said to himself, "Cardinal Monticelso, I will not trust thee, but in all my plots I'll rest as suspicious as a besieged town. Thou cannot reach to and comprehend what I intend to act. Your flax soon kindles, and soon it is out again, but gold slowly heats, and long will it remain hot."

Francisco de Medici had every intention of getting revenge against Brachiano, but he was willing to wait for his revenge.

Cardinal Monticelso returned, carrying the black-book.

He said, "Here it is, my lord."

Francisco de Medici said, "First, your intelligencers — your spies and informants. Please, let me see their names."

Cardinal Monticelso turned to a section of the black-book and said, "Their number increases strangely, and some of them you'd take for honest men."

He turned to other sections of the black-book and said, "Next are panders.

"These are pirates.

"And these following leaves are for base rogues who ruin young gentlemen, by taking up commodities."

The commodity swindle was a way to get around laws against usury. A young gentleman would need a loan, and an unscrupulous lender would sell commodities — goods — to the young gentleman to sell. The young gentleman would sell the commodities for much less than the amount of the loan, but he would be required to pay back the full amount of the loan.

Cardinal Monticelso said, "And these leaves are for politic bankrupts."

Some people would borrow money, pretend to go bankrupt, and then settle with the lenders for pennies on the dollar.

Cardinal Monticelso said, "And these leaves are for fellows who are bawds to their own wives, only to put off horses, and slight jewels, clocks, defaced plate, and such commodities, at the birth of their first children."

Some husbands would allow their wives to have an affair, but after the birth of the first bastard would sell commodities at high prices to the man who had cuckolded him. The adulterous man would buy the commodities in order to keep the husband quiet about the affair — in this society, adultery was scandalous and punishable by law.

Francisco de Medici asked, "Are there really such men?"

Cardinal Monticelso nodded and then continued, "These leaves are for impudent bawds who go in men's apparel."

Some female prostitutes worn men's clothing.

Cardinal Monticelso continued, "These leaves are for usurers who share with scriveners for their good reportage."

Scriveners would recommend a certain usurer for clients who needed to borrow money. In return for their good recommendation that steered borrowers to the usurer, the scriveners received a payment from the usurer.

Cardinal Monticelso continued, "These leaves are for lawyers who will antedate their writs."

A writ might command someone to do something within a certain time. If the writ were antedated, they would have less time to do it and so might end up violating the law.

Cardinal Monticelso continued, "And some divines you might find enfolded there in these leaves, except that I skip over them for conscience's sake.

"Here in these leaves is a general catalogue of knaves: A man might study all the prisons over, yet never attain this knowledge."

Francisco de Medici said, "Murderers? Fold down the leaf that lists murderers, please.

"My good lord, let me borrow this strange doctrine."

Cardinal Monticelso handed him the book and said, "Please use it, my lord."

Francisco de Medici replied, "I do assure your lordship, you are a worthy member of the state, and have done infinite good in your discovery of these offenders."

Cardinal Monticelso said, "Somewhat, sir."

He meant: Some, but not infinite, good.

Francisco de Medici said, "Oh, God! Better than tribute of wolves paid in England — it will hang their skins on the hedge."

In order to control the wolf population in Wales, King Edgar of England imposed a tribute of 300 wolves per year on the Welsh.

The skins of animals could be hung on hedges and dried in the sun. The tribute of wolves would be paid in 300 wolf-skins.

The black-book that listed so many criminals could assist in punishing them. The criminals' skin would figuratively be hung on the hedge.

Cardinal Monticelso said, "I must make bold to leave your lordship."

Francisco de Medici said, "Dearly, sir, I thank you. If anyone asks for me at court, report that you have left me in the company of knaves."

The knaves were listed in the book, but soon he would make use of at least one of those knaves.

Cardinal Monticelso exited.

Now alone, Francisco de Medici said to himself, "I gather now by this, some cunning fellow who is my lord's — Cardinal Monticelso's — officer, and who lately skipped from a clerk's desk up to a justice's chair, has made this knavish summons, and intends, as the Irish rebels were accustomed to sell heads, likewise to make a profit from these."

Heads can be sold when someone puts a bounty on the heads of those people they want killed.

Francisco de Medici continued, "And thus it — making a profit from this black-book of names — happens: Your poor rogues pay for it, poor rogues who haven't the means to present a bribe in their fist; the rest of the band are razed out of the knaves' record or else my lord the cardinal winks at them with easy will. His man grows rich, and the knaves are the knaves still.

"But as for the use I'll make of it, it shall serve to point me out a list of murderers, agents for my villainy.

"If I wanted ten leash — ten sets of three — of courtesans, this black-book would furnish me. Indeed, I could equip three armies with laundresses of easy virtue.

"I marvel that in so little paper should lie the undoing of so many men! It is not as big as twenty official proclamations.

"See the corrupted use that some people make of books. Books of divinity — when in interpretations by some bloodthirsty faction they are wrested away from advocating peace — draw swords, swell battles, and overthrow all good.

"To fashion my revenge more seriously, let me remember my dear sister's face. Call for her picture? No, I'll close my eyes, and in a melancholic thought I'll frame her image before me."

Melancholic people were thought to have strong imaginations.

Francisco de Medici closed his eyes, and Isabella's ghost entered the room.

He said, "Now I have her image fixed in my mind."

He opened his eyes, saw his sister's ghost, and cursed, "By God's foot!"

Recovering from his shock, he said, "How strongly imagination works! How imagination can frame images of things that are not! I think she stands before me, and by the quick idea of my mind, if my artistic skill was creative and fertile, I could draw her picture.

"Thought, like a subtle conjuror, makes us deem things to be supernatural that actually have a cause as common as sickness. It is my melancholy, the result of an excess of black bile, that causes me to see this ghost."

He asked Isabella's ghost, "How came thou by thy death?"

But immediately he said to himself, "How foolish I am to question my own foolishness! Did a man ever dream while awake until now?

"Remove this object! Out of my brain with it! What have I to do with tombs, or death-beds, funerals, or tears — I who have to meditate upon revenge?"

Isabella's ghost exited.

Alone again, Francisco de Medici said to himself, "So, now it is ended, like an old wife's tale. Statesmen think often they see stranger sights than madmen.

"Come, let me return to this serious and weighty business. My tragedy must have some idle mirth in it, or else it will never be accepted by an audience."

He thought of the idle mirth he would use in the tragedy: "I am in 'love,' in 'love' with Vittoria Corombona; and my lovesuit thus halts to her in verse."

He wrote a love poem to her. The lines of the love poem were bad; they were written in halting verse.

Having finished writing the poem, Francisco de Medici began to seal it and said, "I have done it splendidly. Oh, the fate of princes! I am so used to frequent flattery, that, being alone, I now flatter myself. But it will serve. It is now sealed."

A servant entered the room and Francisco de Medici said, "Bear this letter to the House of Convertites, and watch for an opportunity to give it to the hands of Vittoria Corombona, or to the Matron, when some followers of Brachiano are nearby. Leave!"

Carrying the sealed letter, the servant exited.

Francisco de Medici said, "He who deals only by the use of strength, his wit is shallow. When a man's head goes through, each limb will follow."

A proverb stated, "When a fox' head goes through, each limb will follow."

He continued, "The instrument for my business will be bold Count Lodovico.

"It is gold that must such an instrument procure.
"With an empty fist no man does falcons lure.
"Brachiano, I am now fit for thy encounter:
"Like the wild Irish, I'll never think thee dead
"Till I can play at football with thy head,
"*Flectere si nequeo superos, Acheronta movebo*."

The first soccer (British football) ball was a severed human head.

The Latin words mean, "If I cannot prevail upon the gods above, I will move hell."

The Matron of the House of Convertites and Flamineo spoke together.

The Matron said, "Should it be known that the Duke of Brachiano has such access to your imprisoned sister, Vittoria, I would be likely to incur much damage because of it."

"Not a scruple," Flamineo said. "Not even a tiny bit. The Pope lies on his deathbed, and the heads of those who could cause you trouble are troubled now with other business than the guarding of a lady."

Francisco de Medici's servant, carrying Francisco's letter, entered the scene and said, "Flamineo is yonder in conference with the Matron."

He walked over to them and said to the Matron, "Let me speak with you. I entreat you to deliver for me this letter to the fair Vittoria."

"I shall, sir," the Matron said.

Brachiano entered the scene.

Francisco de Medici's servant said, "Deliver it with all care and secrecy. Hereafter you shall know me, and you shall receive thanks for this courtesy."

Francisco de Medici's servant exited.

Flamineo said, "What's going on now? What's that?"

"A letter," the Matron answered.

"To my sister?" Flamineo said. "I'll see that it is delivered."

The Matron handed him the letter and then exited.

Flamineo looked at the letter.

Brachiano asked, "What's that you are reading, Flamineo?"

"Look," Flamineo said, handing him the letter.

Brachiano looked at it and said, "Ha!"

He read out loud, "*To the most unfortunate, his best respected Vittoria.*"

He then asked, "Who was the messenger who brought this letter?"

"I don't know," Flamineo answered.

"No!" Brachiano said. "Who sent it?"

Flamineo cursed, "By God's foot! You speak as if a man should know what fowl is coffined in a baked meat-pie before you cut it up."

Brachiano said, "I'll open it, and I would open it even if it were her heart. What's here subscribed! It's signed by the Duke of Florence, Francisco de Medici! This deception is gross and palpable. I have found out who sent it here."

He handed Flamineo the letter and said, "Read it, read it."

Flamineo read out loud:

"*Your tears I'll turn to triumphs, be but mine;*

"*Your prop is fallen: I pity, that a vine*

"*Which princes heretofore have longed to gather,*

"*Wanting [Lacking] supporters, now should fade and wither.*"

In the poem, Francisco de Medici was comparing Vittoria to a vine. The prop that had fallen and no longer supported her was Brachiano.

Flamineo commented to Brachiano, "Wine, indeed, my lord, with lees — dregs — would serve Francisco de Medici's turn."

He read out loud:

"*Your sad imprisonment I'll soon uncharm,*

"*And with a princely uncontrolled arm*

"*Lead you to Florence, where my love and care*

"*Shall hang your wishes in my silver hair.*"

Flamineo commented, "A halter on his strange equivocation!"

Flamineo may have realized immediately that the letter was a trick by Francisco de Medici to make Brachiano jealous. If so, he also may have realized immediately that Francisco de Medici was not in love with Vittoria. That being the case, Francisco de Medici very likely would want Vittoria punished. The word "hang" would in that case mean hang by a noose, which this society called a halter.

Flamineo read out loud:

"*Nor for my years return me the sad willow;*

"*Who would prefer blossoms before fruit that's mellow?*"

Francisco de Medici was asking not to be rejected because of his silver hair and his age.

Willows were a symbol of unrequited love.

Mellow fruit is ripe fruit. Francisco de Medici believed that ripe, sweet, juicy fruit was preferable to blossoms.

Flamineo commented, "The fruit is rotten, on my knowledge, with lying too long in the bedstraw."

Fruit was laid in straw while it ripened. Straw was also used in mattresses.

Flamineo read out loud:

"*And all the lines of age this line convinces;*

"*The gods never wax [grow] old, no more do princes.*"

The "lines of age" meant 1) wrinkles on his face, and 2) old maxims and proverbs.

Princes never grow old? If they don't (of course, some do grow old), a cynic might say that it's because they are assassinated before they grow old.

But the line can be interpreted as saying that princes never grow older than the gods, which is true because the gods are immortal.

Flamineo commented, "A pox on it! Tear the letter to pieces. Let's have no more atheists, for God's sake."

He was saying that Francisco de Medici was an atheist because he had mentioned the ancient gods, plural, rather than the god of Christianity.

Brachiano cursed, "By God's death! I'll cut Vittoria into motes of dust, and let the irregular, disorderly north wind sweep her up and blow her into Francisco de Medici's nostrils. Where's this whore?"

"This whore" was Vittoria, Flamineo's sister.

"What?" Flamineo said. "What do you call her?"

"Oh, I could be mad!" Brachiano said. "I could forestall the baldness caused by the cursed disease syphilis that she'll bring me to and tear my own hair off. Where's this changeable stuff?"

By "changeable stuff," Brachiano meant "an inconstant whore," but Flamineo punned on the phrase's other meaning of "changeable material." Some fabrics such as shot silk changed colors when viewed from different directions because the warp-threads were one color and the weft-threads were a different color. Watered silk was a fabric that had a rippled pattern resembling waves and a glossy finish.

Flamineo replied, "Over head and ears in water, I assure you. She is not for your wearing."

One meaning of "over head and ears in water" was that Vittoria was "in deep trouble." Another meaning may be that Vittoria was crying because she was imprisoned.

One meaning of "not for your wearing" is "not for you to have sex with." The proverb "win her and wear her" meant "marry her and consummate the marriage."

Brachiano said, "In, you pander!"

He meant: Go in and get Vittoria, you pander!

Flamineo said, "What, me, my lord? Am I your dog?"

Brachiano said, "A bloodhound."

A bloodhound is a seeker after a fugitive.

Brachiano added, "Do you defy me? Do you resist me? Do you withstand me?"

Flamineo said, "'stand you! Let those who have diseases run; I need no plasters."

Suppurating sores run.

Plasters are bandages.

Brachiano asked, "Do you want to be kicked?"

Flamineo asked, "Do you want to have your neck broken?"

This is how Flamineo had murdered Camillo, Vittoria's husband. Someone who has murdered once is capable of murdering twice.

Flamineo continued, "I tell you, Duke Brachiano, I am not in Russia. My shins must be kept whole."

Russians were reputed to hurt the shins of a person who had the money needed to pay off a debt but who refused to pay.

Brachiano asked, "Do you know who I am?"

"Oh, my lord, thoroughly!" Flamineo replied. "As in this world there are degrees of evils, so in this world there are degrees of devils. You're a great duke, and I'm your poor secretary. I look now for a Spanish fig, or an Italian salad, daily."

He meant that he looked to be poisoned soon. The poison could be put in a Spanish fig or an Italian salad.

Brachiano said, "Pander, ply your convoy, and leave your prating."

"Pander, ply your convoy" meant "get on with your business as pandar." The convoy was a person being escorted: Vittoria. Brachiano still wanted Flamineo to go in and get Vittoria.

Flamineo said, "All your kindness to me is like that miserable courtesy of Polyphemus to Ulysses; you reserve me to be devoured last."

In Homer's *Odyssey*, Odysseus (his Roman name is Ulysses) and some of his men visited the cave of Polyphemus the one-eyed Cyclops, who immediately ate two of Odysseus' men. After Odysseus gave him some wine, Polyphemus gave Odysseus a guest-gift: He would eat Odysseus last.

Flamineo continued, "You would dig turfs out of my grave to feed your larks; that would be music to you.

"Come, I'll lead you to her."

Flamineo walked inside backwards, facing Brachiano, who followed him.

Brachiano said, "Do you face me?"

One meaning of "face" was "look threateningly at."

Flamineo replied, "Oh, sir, I would not go before a politic — crafty and devious — enemy with my back towards him, even if there were a whirlpool behind me."

In Homer's *Odyssey*, Odysseus must choose to sail between Scylla and Charybdis. The enchantress Circe tells him, "Scylla is a man-eating monster with twelve legs and six necks. If you sail too close to Scylla, she will shoot her six long necks out of the cavern she lives in, and each of her mouths will seize a man to devour. Charybdis is a whirlpool. If you sail too close to Charybdis, it will suck your ship down into the ocean and destroy it. It is better to sail close to Scylla. You will lose six men, but you will not lose your entire ship and all the men on board."

Once Brachiano and Flamineo were inside, Vittoria came over to them.

Brachiano said to her, "Can you read, mistress? Look upon that letter."

He handed her the letter and continued, "There are no strange characters, nor hieroglyphics. You need no commentary to understand it; I have grown to be your pimp and receive your love-letters.

"By God's precious blood! You shall be a splendid great lady, a stately and advanced-in-society whore."

Vittoria asked, "What are you saying, sir?"

Brachiano said, "Come, come, let's see your cabinet, discover your treasury of love-letters. Death and Furies! I'll see them all."

Vittoria replied, "Sir, upon my soul, I haven't any love-letters. From where was this letter sent?"

Brachiano said, "Confusion on your politic — faked — ignorance! You are reclaimed, are you? I'll give you the bells, and let you fly to the devil."

A reclaimed hawk was a tamed hawk. Reclaimed hawks had bells attached to their legs.

Brachiano was saying that Vittoria was untamed and evil, and he would just give her the bells and let her fly to the devil rather than seek to tame her.

Flamineo warned, "Beware of the hawk, my lord."

Looking at the letter, Vittoria said, "The Duke of Florence! This is some treacherous plot, my lord. To me he never was lovely, I say, so much as in my sleep."

The words were ambiguous. If she slept soundly, without dreaming, then she would not think of the Duke of Florence at all. But if she dreamed of him while she was sleeping, then his loveliness in real life never equaled or surpassed the loveliness he had in her dreams.

Brachiano said, "Right! There are plots. Your beauty! Oh, ten thousand curses on it! How long have I beheld the devil in crystal!"

"Beholding the devil in crystal" was a proverbial saying meaning "being deceived." Think of fake fortune tellers looking at a 'devil' inside a crystal ball.

He continued, "Thou have led me, like a heathen sacrifice, with music, and with fatal yokes of flowers, to my eternal ruin. Woman to man is either a god, or a wolf."

Vittoria began, "My lord —"

Brachiano said, "Go away! We'll be as differing as two magnets — the one shall shun the other. What! Do thou weep?

"Procure but ten of thy dissembling trade, and you'd furnish all the Irish funerals with howling beyond-wild Irish."

At the funerals of wealthy people in Ireland, professional Irish mourners were hired to loudly mourn.

Flamineo said, "Bah, my lord!"

Brachiano said about Vittoria's hand, "That hand, that cursed hand, which I have wearied with doting kisses!"

Thinking of his late wife, Isabella, whose murder he had caused, he said, "Oh, my sweetest duchess, how lovely are thou now!"

He said to Vittoria, "Thy loose thoughts scatter like mercury."

When a ball of mercury is pressed, it divides into smaller balls and scatters. Mercury is sometimes called quicksilver because it looks like silver and quickly moves.

Brachiano continued, "I was bewitched, for all the world speaks ill of thee."

Vittoria said, "No matter. I'll live in such a way now that I'll make that world recant, and change her speeches."

She then said, "You did name your duchess."

Brachiano said, "Whose death may God pardon!"

Vittoria said, "Whose death may God revenge on thee, most godless duke!"

Flamineo said to himself, "Now for two whirlwinds going at each other."

Vittoria said to Brachiano, "What have I gained by thee, but infamy? Thou have stained the spotless honor of my family, and thou have frightened noble society away from my family, who are like those who are sick with the palsy, and retain stinking foxes about them, and are always shunned by those of choicer nostrils."

The stinking foxes were thought to be effective against the disease called palsy, but the treatment caused the person suffering from the palsy to stink like the foxes.

Vittoria continued, "What do you call this house? Is this your palace? Didn't the judge call it a house of penitent whores? Who sent me to it? Who sent me to this incontinent college? Wasn't it you? Isn't this your high promotion in society for me? Go, go and brag about how many ladies you have ruined, like me.

"Fare you well, sir; let me hear no more of you! I had a limb corrupted with an ulcer, but I have cut it off; and now I'll go weeping to heaven on crutches."

The ulcerous leg was her relationship with Brachiano, but she was saying she had just ended that.

Mark 9:45 states, "*And if thy foot offend thee, cut it off: it is better for thee to enter halt into life, than having two feet to be cast into hell, into the fire that never shall be quenched*" (King James Version).

She continued, "As for your gifts, I will return them all, and I wish that I could make you the full executor of all my sins. Oh, that I could toss myself into a grave as quickly! For all thou are worth, I'll not shed one tear more — I'll burst first."

She threw herself upon a bed.

Brachiano said, "I have drunk from the Lethe River."

The Lethe River is the river of forgetfulness.

He said, "Vittoria! My dearest happiness! Vittoria! What do you ail, my love? Why do you weep?"

Vittoria said, "Yes, I now weep poniards, do you see?"

Poniards are daggers.

Each teardrop stabbed, but did it stab Vittoria, Brachiano, or both?

Brachiano asked, "Are not those matchless eyes mine?"

Vittoria replied, "I had rather they were not matches."

If they were not matched, she might be ugly. She preferred being ugly to being Brachiano's.

Brachiano asked, "Is not this lip mine?"

Turning away from him, Vittoria replied, "Yes; thus I would rather bite it off, rather than give it to thee."

Flamineo advised, "Turn to my lord, good sister."

Vittoria replied, "Go away from here, you pander!"

"Pander!" Flamineo said. "Am I the author of your sin?"

"Yes," Vittoria replied. "He's a base thief who a thief lets in."

Flamineo had let Brachiano into her life.

Flamineo said to Brachiano, "We're blown up, my lord —"

It was as if a mine had exploded under them.

Brachiano asked Vittoria, "Will thou listen to me? Once to be jealous of thee is to express that I will love thee everlastingly and never more be jealous."

Vittoria replied, "Oh, thou fool, whose greatness has by much overgrown thy intelligence! What dare thou do that I don't dare to suffer, excepting to be always thy whore? As for my being thy whore, in the sea's bottom sooner thou shall make a bonfire."

Flamineo said, "Oh, no oaths, for God's sake!"

Brachiano asked, "Will you listen to me?"

Vittoria said, "Never."

Flamineo said, "What a damned abscess is a woman's will! Can nothing break it?"

He said to Brachiano, "Bah, bah, my lord, women are caught as you take tortoises — she must be turned on her back."

She would be in the missionary position.

Flamineo said to Vittoria, "Sister, by this hand I am on your side."

He said to Brachiano, "Come, come, you have wronged her. What a strange credulous man you were, my lord, to think the Duke of Florence would love her! Will any mercer — dealer in fine fabrics — take another's ware once it has been roughly handled and sullied?"

He said to Vittoria, "And yet, sister, how scurvily this recalcitrance and naughtiness become you! Young rabbits stand against the hunters not long, and women's anger should, like their flight, procure a little sport: a full cry for a quarter of an hour, and then be put to the dead squat."

A cry is 1) the shedding of tears, and 2) the sound made by hounds in the hunt.

A dead squat is the squatting position taken by an animal at bay or in hiding.

An animal at bay will either kill its attacker or attackers, or it will die. In the case of a young rabbit, it will almost certainly huddle in fright and then be killed.

In this society, "to die" meant to have an orgasm.

Brachiano asked, "Shall these eyes, which have for so long a time dwelt upon your face, be now put out?"

Flamineo said to his sister, "No cruel landlady in the world, who lends forth pennies to street-cleaners, and takes interest for the loans, would do it."

He said to Brachiano, "Caress her, my lord, and kiss her. Don't be like a ferret, to let go your hold with blowing."

Ferrets were supposed to release whatever they had captured if you blew on their face.

Brachiano said, "Let us renew right hands."

A man and a woman who held hands and made vows to each other would be betrothed. Often, the man would place a ring on the woman's right hand, and during the marriage ceremony later the ring would be placed on the left hand. Apparently, Brachiano and Vittoria had previously held hands and made vows to each other.

Vittoria yelled, "Get out!"

Brachiano said, "Never shall rage, or the wine that makes one forget, make me commit such a fault."

Flamineo said to him, "Now you are on the right track — follow it hard!"

Brachiano said to Vittoria, "As long as thou are at peace with me, I don't care if all the rest of the world threaten me with violent cannon."

Flamineo said to his sister, "Note his penitence. The best natures do commit the grossest faults, when they're given over to jealousy, just as the best wine, dying, makes the strongest vinegar.

"I'll tell you: The sea's more rough and raging than calm rivers, but not so sweet, nor so wholesome.

"A quiet woman is a still water under a great bridge. A man may shoot her safely."

At times, it is very difficult to sail under London Bridge. Doing so quickly is called shooting.

Another meaning of the verb "shoot" is "ejaculate into."

Vittoria said, "Oh, you dissembling men!"

Flamineo replied, "We sucked that, sister, from women's breasts, in our first infancy."

He meant that men had imbibed dissembling with their mother's milk when they were infants.

Vittoria said, "To add misery to misery!"

Brachiano said, "Sweetest!"

"Am I not low enough?" Vittoria said. "Aye, aye, your good heart gathers and grows bigger like a snowball rolls and becomes bigger, now that your affection's cold."

She was saying that he didn't love her anymore, and so he was acting more in accordance with his good heart, which preferred to reject her. Despite his words, she still did not believe that he loved her.

Flamineo said to her, "By God's foot, it shall melt into a heart again, or all the wine in Rome shall run down to the dregs for it."

Vittoria said to Brachiano, "Your dog or hawk should be rewarded better than I have been. I'll speak not one word more."

The reward for a dog or a hawk after hunting was a part of the prey it killed.

Flamineo said to Brachiano, "Stop her mouth with a sweet kiss, my lord."

Brachiano kissed Vittoria.

Flamineo said to his sister, "So, now the tide's turned, the vessel's come about. Brachiano is facing in the right direction again. He's a sweet armful. Oh, we curl-haired men are always very kind to women! This is well."

Brachiano said to Vittoria, "That you should chide like this!"

Flamineo said to Brachiano, "Oh, sir, little chimneys always cast the most smoke! I sweat for you. Couple together with as deep a silence as did the Grecians in their wooden horse."

"Couple together" can mean 1) be together, or 2) have sex together. Since sex can be noisy, Flamineo probably was advising Brachiano to continue to tightly hug Vittoria. The sex can come later.

In Virgil's *Aeneid*, the Greeks finally conquered Troy with a trick. They built a huge hollow horse, filled it with soldiers, and left it behind as they pretended to sail away. They also left behind a Greek, who pretended to have escaped from them in order to avoid capital punishment, to tell the Trojans that if the wooden horse were taken inside Troy, the city would never fall. The Trojans took the wooden horse inside Troy, and that night, after remaining very quiet for a long time, the Greek soldiers came out of the horse, went to the city gates, and opened them to let the Greek army inside the city.

Flamineo continued, "My lord, supply your promises with deeds. You know that painted food no hunger feeds."

Painted still lifes of fruit feed no one.

Flamineo had done his job: He had reconciled his sister and Brachiano. Now — or soon — he wanted to be rewarded.

Referring to Flamineo as Rome, Brachiano said, "Wait, ungrateful Rome —"

Rome was sometimes ungrateful to the people who served it, so Brachiano might more accurately be compared to Rome. One example is Coriolanus, a hero whom the Romans exiled.

Flamineo said, "Rome! It deserves to be called Barbary, on account of the villainous way it treats us."

Barbary was a land of barbarians.

Brachiano said, "Quiet! The same project that the Duke of Florence (whether because of love for Vittoria or as an attempt to fool us I don't know) laid down for her escape, I will pursue."

He was going to take Vittoria from the House of Convertites. In his letter, part of which had not been read out loud, the Duke of Florence had outlined an escape plan for Vittoria.

Flamineo said, "And there is no time fitter than this night, my lord. Because the Pope is dead, and all the cardinals have entered the conclave for electing a new Pope, the city is in a great confusion. We may clothe her in a page's suit, arrange a series of post-horses, embark on a ship, and sail as quickly as we can for Padua."

Brachiano said, "I'll immediately steal away the Prince Giovanni, and make for Padua. You two with your old mother, and young Marcello who serves the Duke of Florence — if you can convince Marcello to join us — will follow me. I will advance — promote — you all; as for you, Vittoria, think of a duchess' title."

He would marry her.

Flamineo said, "Did you hear that, sister!"

He then said to Brachiano, "Wait, my lord; I'll tell you a tale.

"The crocodile, which lives in the Nile River, has a worm that breeds in its teeth, which puts it to extreme anguish. A little bird, no bigger than a wren, is barber-surgeon — a dentist — to this crocodile. It flies into the crocodile's jaw, picks out the worm, and brings immediate relief. The aquatic reptile, glad of ease, but ungrateful to her that gave the ease, so that the bird may not talk widely about the crocodile abroad because of non-payment for the service rendered, closes its jaws, intending to swallow the bird, and so put the bird to perpetual silence. But nature, loathing such ingratitude, has armed this bird with a quill or prick on the head, the top of which wounds the crocodile in the mouth, thereby forcing the crocodile to open its bloody prison, and away flies the pretty tooth-picker from her cruel patient."

Brachiano said, "Your meaning is that I have not rewarded the service you have done for me."

True, but Flamineo cunningly provided another plausible interpretation of the tale.

Flamineo replied, "No, my lord."

He then said to Vittoria, "You, sister, are the crocodile. You are blemished in your reputation, my lord cures it; and though the comparison does not hold in every particular, yet observe, and remember, what good the bird with the prick in the head has done for you, and scorn ingratitude."

He was saying that Brachiano was going to cure her bad reputation by marrying her, and therefore Vittoria ought to be grateful to him.

Flamineo then thought:

It may appear to some ridiculous
Thus to talk knave and madman, and sometimes
Come in with a dried [old] sentence [aphorism], stuffed with sage [wisdom]:
But this allows my varying of shapes;
Knaves do grow great by being great men's apes.

Flamineo knew that many people would find his behavior ridiculous, but there was a reason for his behavior. By serving Brachiano, he was hoping to rise and grow great.

Francisco de Medici met Lodovico, Gasparo, and six ambassadors. Lodovico and Gasparo were escorting the six ambassadors as they came from the conclave to elect a new pope. Some other people were present.

Francisco de Medici said to Lodovico, "So, my lord, I commend your diligence. Guard well the conclave, and as the order is, let none have conversation with the cardinals."

No conversation was permitted because the cardinals ought not to be bothered for appeals to elect one or another cardinal to be the new pope.

Lodovico replied, "I shall, my lord."

He then ordered some of the people around the ambassadors, "Make room for the ambassadors."

Gasparo said, "They're wondrously and splendidly dressed today. Why do they wear these different kinds of clothing?"

Lodovico said, "Oh, sir, the ambassadors are knights of several orders:

"That lord in the black cloak, with the silver cross, is Knight of Rhodes.

"The next is Knight of St. Michael.

"That ambassador is Knight of the Golden Fleece.

"The Frenchman, there, is Knight of the Holy Ghost.

"My Lord of Savoy is Knight of the Annunciation.

"The Englishman is Knight of the honored Garter, dedicated to their saint, St. George.

"I could describe to you their different institutions, with the laws annexed to their orders, except that time does not permit such a discourse."

Francisco de Medici asked, "Where's Count Lodovico?"

Lodovico answered, "Here, my lord."

Francisco de Medici said, "It is on the point of dinner time. Marshal the cardinals' service."

Lodovico replied, "Sir, I shall."

Several servants entered the room, carrying covered dishes.

Lodovico ordered a servant, "Wait, let me examine your dish. Who is this for?"

The servant replied, "For my Lord Cardinal Monticelso."

Lodovico asked another servant, "Whose is this?"

The second servant replied, "For my Lord Cardinal of Bourbon."

Lodovico examined each covered dish.

The French Ambassador asked, "Why does he examine the dishes? To observe what food has been prepared?"

The English Ambassador answered, "No, sir, he examines them to prevent any letters being conveyed in to bribe or to solicit the advancement of any cardinal.

"When first they enter the conclave, it is lawful for the ambassadors of princes to enter with them, and to make their suit for any man their prince likes best; but afterward, until a general election is held and the pope has been chosen, no man may speak with them."

Lodovico ordered, "You who attend on the lord cardinals, open the window and receive their food."

A conclavist — a person serving the cardinals as they elected a new pope — opened the window and said, "You must return the service: The lord cardinals are busy about electing the Pope. They have given over scrutiny and are fallen to admiration."

The word "scrutiny" meant examining the votes. When there were not enough votes for one person to become pope, the cardinals fell to adoration: If enough cardinals turned to one cardinal and bowed or kneeled, that cardinal became the new pope. A two-thirds majority was needed for a cardinal to become pope.

Lodovico told the servants carrying covered dishes, "Away, away. Leave, leave."

The servants exited.

Francisco de Medici said, "I'll lay a thousand ducats you hear news of a new pope very quickly."

A clamor sounded.

Francisco de Medici said, "Listen; surely, a new pope's elected.

"Look, my Lord of Arragon appears on the church battlements."

The Lord Cardinal of Arragon proclaimed in Latin:

"*Denuntio vobis gaudium magnum: Reverendissimus Cardinalis Lorenzo de Monticelso electus est in sedem apostolicam, et elegit sibi nomen Paulum Quartum.*"

["I announce to you with great joy: The Most Reverend Cardinal Lorenzo Monticelso has been elected to the Apostolic See, and he chose as the name for himself Paul IV."]

Everyone shouted in Latin: "*Vivat Sanctus Pater Paulus Quartus!*"

["Long live the Holy Father Paul IV!"]

A servant said to Francisco de Medici, "Vittoria, my lord —"

Francisco de Medici quickly asked, "Well, what of her?"

The servant continued, "— has fled the city —"

Francisco de Medici said, "Ha!"

The servant finished, "— with Duke Brachiano."

Francisco de Medici said, "Fled! Where's the Prince Giovanni?"

The servant answered, "Gone with his father: Brachiano."

Francisco de Medici ordered, "Let the Matron of the Convertites be arrested. Fled? Oh, damnable!"

The servant exited.

Francisco de Medici then said, "How fortunate are my wishes! Why, it was for just this I labored: I sent the letter to instruct him what to do."

The letter had included a plan for helping Vittoria escape from the House of the Convertites.

Francisco de Medici continued, "Thy reputation, foolish Duke of Brachiano, I first have poisoned. I directed thee in the way to marry a whore; what can be worse?

"This follows:

"The hand must act to drown the passionate tongue.

"I scorn to wear a sword and prate of wrong."

Francisco de Medici intended to take action to get revenge for the wrongs done to him rather than just complain.

Cardinal Monticelso, who was now Pope Paul IV and who was wearing the special clothing of a pope, arrived and said in Latin, "*Concedimus vobis Apostolicam benedictionem, et remissionem peccatorum.*"

["We grant you the Apostolic blessing and forgiveness of sins."]

Cardinal Monticelso, who was now Pope Paul IV, said, "My lord reports that Vittoria Corombona has stolen away from the House of Convertites by the means of Brachiano, and they have fled the city.

"Now, although this is the first day of our seat, we cannot better please the Divine Power than to sequester from the Holy Church these cursed persons. Make it therefore known that we pronounce excommunication against them both. All who are their family and friends in Rome we likewise banish. Let's go."

Everyone except Francisco de Medici and Lodovico exited.

Francisco de Medici said, "Come, dear Lodovico. Have you taken the sacrament to prosecute the intended murder?"

"With all constancy," Lodovico said. "But, sir, I wonder you'll engage yourself in person, because you are a great prince."

Francisco de Medici said, "Don't divert me from my course of action. Most members of his court are of my faction, and some are of my council. Noble friend, our danger shall be alike in this design. Let part of the glory be mine."

Francisco de Medici took off his cap to honor Lodovico, and then he exited.

Cardinal Monticelso, who was now Pope Paul IV, had returned in time to see Francisco de Medici and Lodovico talking together. He asked Lodovico, "Why did the Duke of Florence with such care labor to bring about your pardon? Tell me."

Lodovico replied, "Italian beggars will explain that to you. These Italian beggars, begging for alms, order those they beg from, to do good for their own sakes.

"Or it may be that he spreads his bounty with a sowing hand, like kings, who many times give excessively — out of measure — not for desert so much, as for their pleasure."

According to Lodovico's reply, Francisco de Medici brought about the pardon either to do good for his own soul or out of generosity because he possessed so much wealth.

The newly elected Pope Paul IV said, "I know you're cunning. Come, what devil was that you were raising?"

One meaning of the word "cunning" is "knowledgeable in occult matters."

Lodovico asked, "Devil, my lord?"

The newly elected Pope Paul IV said, "I ask you, how does the Duke of Florence employ you? What do you do that caused his hat to fall to his knee with such compliment to you, when he departed from you?"

Lodovico said, "Why, my lord, he told me of a resty, sluggish, inactive Barbary horse that he would have liked to bring to the career, the sault, and the ring galliard."

The metaphorical Barbary horse was Vittoria. The career, the sault, and the ring galliard were all actions that a good trainer taught a horse.

Lodovico said, "Now, my lord, I have a rare French rider."

The French had an international reputation for riding well on horseback.

Riding well means giving the horse commands and having the commands obeyed.

The metaphorical French rider was Francisco de Medici, who gave Lodovico commands that Lodovico had promised to obey.

The newly elected Pope Paul IV said, "Take your heed, lest the jade break your neck."

A jade can be 1) a bad horse, or 2) a bad woman.

He continued, "Do you put me off with your wild horse-tricks? Sirrah, you lie.

"Oh, thou are a foul black cloud, and thou threaten to be a violent storm!"

Lodovico replied, "Storms are in the air, my lord; I am too low to storm."

He was a count, but dukes and popes ranked higher.

The newly elected Pope Paul IV said, "Wretched creature! I know that thou are fashioned for all ill, like dogs. Once dogs get blood, they'll always kill.

"The talk you and Francisco de Medici had was about some murder, wasn't it?"

Lodovico replied, "I'll not tell you."

He paused, thought, and then said, "And yet I don't care greatly if I do, indeed, with this condition.

"Holy father, I come to you not as an informant and spy, but as a penitent sinner. What I utter is completely in confession, which, as you know, must never be revealed."

This is true: What is said in confession must never be revealed.

The newly elected Pope Paul IV said, "You have gotten the better of me."

Lodovico said, "Sir, I did love Brachiano's duchess — the late Isabella — dearly, or rather I pursued — attended — her with hot lust, although she never knew about it. She was poisoned — I swear upon my soul she was poisoned. And I have sworn to avenge her murder."

The way he could avenge her murder was to murder Brachiano. To do that, he would have to travel to Padua, where Brachiano was.

The newly elected Pope Paul IV asked, "You have sworn this to the Duke of Florence?"

"To him I have," Lodovico replied.

The newly elected Pope Paul IV said, "Miserable creature! If thou persist in this, it is damnable.

"Do thou imagine that thou can slide on blood, and not be tainted with a shameful fall?

"Or, like the black and melancholic yew-tree, do thou think thou can root thyself in dead men's graves, and yet prosper?

"Instruction to thee comes like sweet showers to over-hardened ground: They wet, but don't pierce deep.

"And so I leave thee, with all the furies hanging around thy neck, until by thy penitence thou remove this evil, by conjuring from thy breast that cruel devil."

The newly elected Pope Paul IV exited.

People in this society took eternal damnation seriously.

Lodovico said to himself, "I'll give it up; I won't commit murder. He says that it is damnable.

"Besides, I expected his support, by reason of the death of Camillo, his nephew."

Francisco de Medici and a servant had arrived a few minutes earlier. Francisco de Medici had seen the newly elected Pope Paul IV and Lodovico talking together, and he worried that Pope Paul IV had said something that might cause Count Lodovico to lose his resolve to murder Brachiano.

Francisco de Medici asked the servant, "Do you know that count?"

"Yes, my lord," the servant replied.

Francisco de Medici ordered, "Carry for him these thousand ducats to his lodging. Tell him the newly elected pope has sent them. Perhaps that will confirm more than all the rest. Perhaps the money will outweigh any words that have been spoken."

He gave the servant the money and then exited.

The servant went over to Lodovico and said, "Sir."

Lodovico asked, "Are you talking to me, sir?"

The servant said, "His Holiness has sent you a thousand crowns, and he wants you, if you travel, to make him your patron for intelligence."

Sometimes, people such as popes or other high-ranking people would subsidize someone's travel as a way to gain information about the countries they were visiting.

Lodovico replied, "I am his creature always to be commanded. I will do what he wants."

He then said to himself, "Why, now it has come about. He vehemently criticized me, and yet these crowns were counted out, and laid ready, before he knew about my voyage.

"Oh, the art, the modest outside appearance of greatness!

"Great ones sit, like brides at wedding-dinners, with their looks turned away from the least wanton jests, their weak stomach sick of the modesty, when their thoughts are loose and unchaste, even performing in their imagination those hot and lustful sports that are to ensue about midnight. Such is the new Pope Paul IV's cunning!

"He sounds my depth thus with a golden plummet."

The golden plummet was the thousand ducats.

He continued, "I am doubly armed now."

Lodovico believed that he had the support of both Francisco de Medici and the new Pope Paul IV.

He continued, "Now to the bloody act of murder.

"There's only three Furies found in spacious hell,

"But in a great man's breast three thousand dwell."

The three avenging goddesses known as the Furies were Tisiphone, Megaera, and Alecto.

The furies in a great man's breast are things such as murderous thoughts.

CHAPTER 5

— 5.1 —

In Padua, Brachiano, Flamineo, Marcello, Hortensio, Vittoria Corombona, Cornelia, Zanche, and others, including the six ambassadors, walked by in a procession. Brachiano and Vittoria had just been married.

Flamineo and Hortensio remained behind as the other members of the procession exited.

Flamineo was the brother of Marcello and Vittoria, and he served as secretary to Brachiano.

Hortensio was one of Brachiano's officers.

"In all the weary minutes of my life, day never dawned until now," Flamineo said. "This marriage confirms me to be a happy man."

Hortensio said, "It is a good assurance of financial and political security."

Flamineo now was brother-in-law to a powerful man: the Duke of Brachiano.

Hortensio asked, "Have you seen yet the Moor who's come to court?"

"Yes," Flamineo said, "and I spoke with him in the Duke of Brachiano's private room. I have not seen a more handsome person, nor have I ever talked with a man better experienced in state affairs or the rudiments of war. He has, according to reports, served the Venetian in Crete these fourteen years, and he has been chief in many a bold military campaign."

"Who are those two who bear him company?" Hortensio asked.

Flamineo answered, "Two noblemen of Hungary, who, living in the emperor's service as commanders, eight years ago, contrary to the expectation of the court, entered into religion, in the strict Order of Capuchins. But being not well settled in their undertaking, they left their Order, and returned to court; for which, being afterward troubled in conscience, they vowed their service against the enemies of Christ, went to Malta, were there knighted, and in their return back, at this great solemnity, they are resolved forever to forsake the world and settle themselves in a house of Capuchins here in Padua."

The Capuchins were an offshoot of the Franciscans.

"It is strange," Hortensio said.

Flamineo said, "One thing makes it so: They have vowed forever to wear, next to their bare bodies, those coats of mail they served in."

Some penitents vowed to wear shirts made of horsehair next to their skin, but these ex-military men would wear armor next to their skin.

"That is a hard penance!" Hortensio said. "Is the Moor a Christian?"

"He is," Flamineo said.

"Why does he offer his service to our duke?" Hortensio asked.

Flamineo answered, "Because he understands there's likely to grow some wars between us and the Duke of Florence, in which he hopes to find employment.

"I never saw one in a stern bold look wear more command, nor in a lofty phrase express more knowing, or deeper contempt of our slight airy courtiers as if he travelled all the princes' courts of Christendom. In all things he strives to express that all who would dispute with him may know that worldly glories, like glow-worms, shine bright from far off, but looked at from a near distance, have neither heat nor light."

He looked up, saw Brachiano coming, and said, "The duke."

Brachiano arrived, along with the three newcomers to the court: the Moor and the two noblemen of Hungary. The newcomers had an attendant with them. Also arriving were Carlo and Pedro and some other attendants.

Events would show that the newcomers to the court were in disguise.

The Moor, who was called Mulinassar, was actually Francisco de Medici in disguise. The two noblemen of Hungary were actually Lodovico and Gasparo in disguise. Antonelli was also in disguise and was serving as an attendant.

Events would also show that Carlo and Pedro, although they served in Brachiano's court, were actually loyal to Francisco de Medici, who had placed them there as informants to him.

Brachiano said to the newcomers, "You are nobly welcome. We have heard fully about your honorable service against the Turk — the Ottoman sultan — our enemy.

"To you, brave Mulinassar, we assign a suitable pension, and we are inwardly sorry that the vows of those two worthy Hungarian gentlemen make them unable to accept our proffered bounty.

"Hungarians, your wish is that you may leave your warlike swords as monuments — tokens of your vow — in our chapel. I accept it as a great honor done to me, and I must ask your leave to contribute your presence during our new duchess' revels.

"Only one thing, as the last vanity — worldly pleasure — you ever shall view, don't leave before seeing a barriers that has been planned for tonight."

A barriers is a kind of martial tournament. Two men would fight with weapons — usually pike and sword — while separated by a waist-high barrier. Larger groups could also fight.

Brachiano continued, "You shall have private standings — you shall have a good place from which to see the contests.

"It has pleased the great ambassadors of several princes, in their return from Rome to their own countries, to grace our marriage, and to honor me with such a kind of sport."

The disguised Francisco de Medici said, "I shall persuade the Hungarians to stay, my lord."

Brachiano said to Flamineo and Hortensio, "Let's set on there to the presence-room."

The presence-room was a room in which a high-ranking person such as a duke received visitors.

Everyone exited except the conspirators against Brachiano.

Carlo said to the disguised Francisco de Medici, "My noble lord, you are most fortunately welcome."

The conspirators embraced.

Carlo added, "You have our vows, sealed with the sacrament, to second your attempts and assist you."

Pedro said, "And all things are ready. Brachiano could not have invented his own ruin (even if he had despaired and committed suicide) with more fitness."

The disguised Lodovico said to the disguised Francisco de Medici, "You would not take my way of dealing with Brachiano."

The disguised Francisco de Medici said, "My way is better ordered."

The disguised Lodovico said, "I would have poisoned his prayer-book, or a set of beads, the pummel of his saddle, his looking-glass or the handle of his tennis racket — oh, I would have poisoned that, that!

"That way, while he had been bandying at tennis, he might have sworn himself to hell, and struck his soul into the hazard!"

The disguised Lodovico wanted to damn Brachiano's soul and not just kill his body. If Brachiano's tennis-racket handle were poisoned, he might play a game, grow angry and swear and die without repenting his sin.

The hazards in tennis were openings in the inner wall where tennis was played.

The disguised Lodovico continued, "Oh, my lord, I would have our plot against Brachiano be ingenious, and have it hereafter recorded as an example to be followed, rather than for us to borrow and follow someone else's example."

The disguised Francisco de Medici said, "There's no way more effective than this way we have already thought through."

The disguised Lodovico said, "Onward, then."

The disguised Francisco de Medici said, "And yet I think that this revenge is poor because it steals upon him like a thief: To instead have taken him by the helmet in a pitched battlefield, led him to Florence —"

The disguised Lodovico interrupted, "It would have been splendid, and there to have crowned him with a wreath of stinking garlic, to have shown the harshness of his government and the rankness of his lust."

He looked up, saw people coming, and said, "Flamineo comes."

The disguised Lodovico, the disguised Gasparo, the disguised Antonelli, Carlo, and Pedro exited, leaving behind the disguised Francisco de Medici, who remained quiet and was not noticed at first by the new arrivals: Flamineo, Marcello, and Zanche.

Flamineo, Marcello, and Vittoria were brothers and sister.

Marcello said, "Tell me why this devil haunts you?"

The devil was Zanche, Vittoria's woman-servant. She was a Moor.

Moors were dark-skinned, and this society regarded the devil as being black.

Flamineo replied, "I don't know. For by this light, I do not conjure for her. It is not so great a cunning as men think, to raise the devil; for here's one up already. The greatest cunning would be to lay him down."

In this context, "cunning" is magic or conjuring.

He was joking. He had put his hands on his crouch and pretended to have an erection as he talked about conjuring the devil down.

"She is your shame," Marcello said.

In this society, dark skin was regarded as ugly.

"I ask thee to pardon her," Flamineo replied. "Truly, you see, women are like burs: Wherever their affection throws them, there they'll stick."

Seeing Francisco de Medici, who was disguised as a Moor, Zanche said, "That is my countryman, a handsome person. When he's at leisure, I'll discourse with him in our own language."

Flamineo said, "I hope you do."

Zanche exited.

Flamineo then said to the disguised Francisco de Medici, "How is it with you, brave soldier? Oh, I wish that I had seen some of your iron days — your days in armor! I ask you to relate some of your military service to us."

The disguised Francisco de Medici replied, "It is a ridiculous thing for a man to be his own chronicler. I did never wash my mouth with my own praise, for fear of getting a stinking breath."

Marcello said, "You're too stoical. The Duke of Brachiano will expect other discourse from you."

The Stoics had a poor opinion of fame. George Long (1800-1879) translated these lines from Book 4 of Marcus Aurelius' *Meditations*:

"He who has a vehement desire for posthumous fame does not consider that every one of those who remember him will himself also die very soon; then again also they who have succeeded them, until the whole remembrance shall have been extinguished as it is transmitted through men who foolishly admire and perish. But suppose that those who will remember are even immortal, and that the remembrance will be immortal, what then is this to thee?"

The disguised Francisco de Medici replied, "I shall never flatter him: I have studied man too much to do that. What difference is between the Duke of Brachiano and me? No more than between two bricks, all made of one and the same kind of clay, only it may be that one brick is placed on top of a tower, and the other brick may be placed in the bottom of a well, by mere chance. If I were placed as high as the duke, I should stick as fast, make as fair a show, and bear out weather equally."

This sounds egalitarian, and the Stoics were in many ways egalitarian, but of course Francisco de Medici and Brachiano were both dukes. The disguised Francisco de Medici was the Duke of Florence. In addition, they were both fair skinned: Under his disguise, Francisco de Medic was light complexioned.

Flamineo said, "If this soldier had a patent to beg in churches, then he would tell them stories."

The soldier was the disguised Francisco de Medici.

Disabled soldiers needed a permit to beg. If they were caught begging without a permit, they could be whipped.

Marcello said, "I have been a soldier, too."

The disguised Francisco de Medici asked, "How have you thrived?"

Marcello replied, "Indeed, poorly."

Previously, Marcello had served Francisco de Medici.

The disguised Francisco de Medici said, "That's the misery of peace: Only outsides are then respected. As ships seem to be very great upon the river, the same ships seem to be very little upon the seas, so some men in the court seem to be Colossuses in a chamber, but the same men, if they came into the battlefield, would appear to be pitiful pigmies."

Flamineo said, "Give me a fair room yet hung with arras, and some great cardinal to lug me by the ears, as his endeared favorite."

An arras is a wall hanging that is often placed in front of an alcove. Behind an arras is often a good place to hide.

The disguised Francisco de Medici said, "And thou may do the devil knows what villainy."

Flamineo said, "And safely."

If he were a cardinal's favorite, he would have a powerful ally.

"Right," the disguised Francisco de Medici said. "You shall see in the country, during harvest-time, pigeons, although they destroy no matter how much corn, the farmer does not dare to present the fowling-piece to them. Why won't the farmer shoot them? Because they belong to the lord of the manor; in the meantime, your poor sparrows, which belong to the Lord of Heaven, go into the cooking-pot for eating the farmer's crops."

"I will now give you some politic instruction," Flamineo said. "The Duke of Brachiano says he will give you pension-money, but that's only a bare promise. Get the promise in a legal contract signed by him. For I have known men who have returned after serving against the Turk: For three or four months they have had pension-money to buy themselves new wooden legs and fresh bandages, but after these three or four months, no pension-money was to be had. And this miserable courtesy is as if a tormentor should give hot cordial drinks to a person who is three-quarters dead on the rack, only to fetch the miserable soul again to endure more dog-days."

The poor soul would be revived only for the purpose of enduring more torture.

Hortensio, Zanche, a young lord, and two other people entered the scene.

Flamineo asked, "How are you now, gallants? Are they ready for the barriers?"

"Yes, " the young lord answered. "The lords are putting on their armor."

The disguised Francisco de Medici exited.

Hortensio asked about him, "Who's he?"

"A new upstart," Flamineo said. "One who swears like a falconer and will lie in the duke's ear day by day, like a maker of almanacs; and yet I have known him, since he came to the court, to smell worse of sweat than an under tennis-court keeper."

Almanacs, which included weather predictions, were regarded as unreliable. Astrologers, who made almanacs, were also often unreliable.

Hortensio said to Flamineo about Zanche, "Look, yonder's your sweet mistress."

Flamineo replied, "Thou are my sworn brother, and so I'll tell thee that I do love that Moor, that witch, very constrainedly."

"Very constrainedly" does not mean "full-heartedly."

He continued, "She knows some of my villainy. I love her just as a man holds a wolf by the ears; except for the fear of her turning upon me, and pulling out my throat, I would let her go to the devil."

A proverb stated, "A man who holds a wolf's ears will be bitten; a man who lets go of the wolf's ears will be killed."

Hortensio said, "I hear she claims marriage from thee."

Flamineo said, "Indeed, I made to her some such dark promise; and, in seeking to fly from it, I run on, like a frightened dog with a bottle at its tail, a dog that would like to bite it off, and yet does not dare to look behind him."

Bottleflies can be dangerous to animals.

Zanche walked over to them, and Flamineo said, "Now, my precious gypsy."

Zanche replied, "Aye, your love to me rather cools than heats."

Flamineo said, "By the Virgin Mary, I am the sounder lover because of it; we have many wenches about the town who heat too fast."

To heat too fast can mean to become lustful too fast, but some sexually transmitted infections cause the sufferer to feel heat in the genital area, legs, and/or buttocks.

Hortensio asked, "What do you think of these perfumed gallants, then?"

Flamineo said, "Their satin cannot save them: I am confident that they have a certain spice — a hint — of the disease, for they who sleep with dogs shall rise with fleas."

The disease is syphilis.

Zanche said, "Believe it, a little paint and gay clothes make you loathe me."

She meant that he would fall or had fallen for a woman wearing makeup and gay clothing and so he did or would hate her.

Flamineo said, "What! Love a lady because of her makeup or gay apparel? I'll unkennel — release — one example more for thee. Aesop had a foolish dog that let go of the flesh in order to attempt to catch the shadow; I would have courtiers be better diners."

Zanche asked, "You remember your oaths?"

Flamineo said, "Lovers' oaths are like mariners' prayers, uttered in extremity; but when the tempest is over, and when the vessel stops tumbling, they fall from protesting — promising — to drinking."

Sailors pray to God and make promises in the middle of a storm when they fear for their lives, but once the storm is over, they go back to their regular practice of drinking.

A woman can be regarded as a vessel, and tumbling can be done in bed. Some men make promises to get a woman in bed, but after the sex is over they forget their promises and go back to drinking.

Flamineo continued, "And yet, among gentlemen, protesting and drinking go together, and agree as well as shoemakers and Westphalia bacon: They are both drawers on."

Westphalia bacon is salted and draws on drink — consuming it incites one to drink — while shoemakers draw on shoes.

Flamineo continued, "For drink draws on protestation, and protestation draws on more drink. Is not this discourse better now than the morality of your sunburnt gentleman?"

The sunburnt gentleman was the disguised Francisco de Medici. Because he was disguising himself as a Moor, he had darkened his face.

Cornelia, the mother of Flamineo, Marcello, and Vittoria, entered the scene, and said to Zanche, "Is this your perch, you haggard? Fly to the stews."

A haggard is a wild female hawk; the stews are brothels.

Cornelia struck Zanche.

Flamineo said, "You should be clapped in irons by the heels now! You have dared to strike in the court!"

Intentionally striking someone hard enough to draw blood in the court was a serious offense that could result in paying a fine, serving time in prison, and having one's right hand cut off.

Cornelia exited.

Zanche said, "She's good for nothing but to make her maids catch cold at nights. They dare not use a bed-staff for fear of her light fingers."

This kind of bed-staff belonged to a man who could keep the serving-women warm at night. Other kinds of bed-staffs were wooden slats laid across bed-stocks and a stick used to assist in making up a bed that had been placed in a recess.

Cornelia's light fingers were employed in striking serving-women. Because she was an old woman, her blows were not heavy.

Marcello said, "You're a strumpet — an impudent one."

He kicked Zanche.

Flamineo asked, "Why do you kick her? Tell me. Do you think that she's like a walnut tree? Must she be beaten before she bears good fruit?"

A proverb stated, "A woman, a dog, and a walnut tree, the more you beat them the better they be." Sometimes, instead of a dog, the proverb mentioned an ass.

Beating a walnut tree makes walnuts fall from the tree. According to the proverb, beating a dog, ass, or woman brings about obedience.

The fruit a woman bears is a baby.

Marcello said, "She brags that you shall marry her."

Flamineo said, "So what?"

Marcello said, "I had rather she were pitched upon a stake, in some new-seeded garden, to frighten her fellow crows away from there."

Flamineo said, "You're a boy, a fool. You be the guardian of your hound. I am of age and need no guardian."

Marcello, who wanted Zanche to stay away from Flamineo, said, "If I take — capture — her near you, I'll cut her throat."

Flamineo asked, "With a fan of feathers?"

Marcello had been a soldier, but now he was in a court: A fan of feathers is something a courtier might possess.

Marcello replied, "And, as for you, I'll whip this folly out of you."

Flamineo asked, "Are you choleric? I'll purge it with rhubarb."

A choleric person is a bad-tempered person.

Hortensio said to Flamineo, "Oh, your brother!"

Flamineo replied, "Hang him! He wrongs me most, he who ought to offend me least."

He then said to his brother, "I suspect my mother played foul play when she conceived thee."

In other words, he was saying that he suspected that their mother had had an affair when she conceived Marcello, and so the two brothers did not have the same father.

Marcello said, "Now, by all my hopes, like the two slaughtered sons of Oedipus, the very flames of our affection shall turn two ways."

Eteocles and Polynices were two brothers — the sons of Oedipus — who agreed to take turns ruling the city of Thebes. One brother was supposed to rule for a year, and then the other brother would rule for a year, and so on. Eteocles ruled for the first year, but then he refused to give up the throne so that his brother could rule for a year. Angry, Polynices gathered an army together and marched against Thebes, creating the story of the Seven Against Thebes. (The Seven were the seven main assailants: one for each of the seven gates of Thebes.) The two brothers killed each other in combat, and when their corpses were cremated together, the flame split in two over their corpses because even in death they were still angry at each other.

Marcello continued, "Those words I'll make thee answer with thy heart-blood."

Flamineo said, "Do, like the geese in the progress. You know where you shall find me."

A progress is a journey undertaken by notables or armies. It would stop at night, and attract a lot of people. Such stops were good places for prostitutes — who were called geese — to conduct business.

Marcello said, "Very good."

Flamineo exited.

Marcello said to the young lord, "If thou are a noble friend, bear him my sword, and ask him to find a sword the length of it."

When people dueled, they would use swords of the same length so that neither had an advantage.

The young lord said, "Sir, I shall."

Everyone except Zanche exited.

Seeing the disguised Francisco de Medici walking toward her, Zanche said, "He is coming! Go away, petty thoughts of my disgrace!"

One disgrace was the way she had been treated by Cornelia and by Marcello.

Another "disgrace" was the color of her skin. This culture did not regard dark complexions as beautiful.

She said to the disguised Francisco de Medici, "I never loved my complexion until now because I may boldly say, without a blush, I love you."

The disguised Francisco de Medici replied, "Your love is untimely sown; there's a spring at Michaelmas, but it is only a faint one. I am sunk in years, and I have vowed never to marry."

Francisco de Medici was middle-aged, while Zanche was young.

Michaelmas is September 29, and in Italy the weather at that time may be spring-like for a while, but only a brief while because colder weather soon sets in.

"Alas!" Zanche said. "Poor maidens get more lovers than husbands, yet you may mistake — underestimate — my wealth. For, as when ambassadors are sent to congratulate princes, there's commonly sent along with them a rich present, so that, although the prince may not like the ambassador's person, nor the ambassador's words, yet he likes well the present. So I may come to you in the same manner, and be better loved for my dowry than for my virtue."

The disguised Francisco de Medici said, "I'll think about the proposal."

"Do," Zanche replied. "I'll now detain you no longer. At your better leisure, I'll tell you things that shall startle your blood:

"Do not blame me because this passion I reveal;

"Lovers die inward when they their flames conceal."

Zanche exited.

Alone, the disguised Francisco de Medici said to himself:
"Of all intelligence this may prove the best:
"Surely I shall draw strange fowl from this foul nest."

Marcello and his mother, Cornelia, talked together. A page was present.

Cornelia said, "I hear a whispering all about the court: You are to fight. Who is your opposite?"

The duel was supposed to be held between Marcello and Flamineo, and so Flamineo was his opposite.

Cornelia also asked, "What is the quarrel about?"

Marcello said, "It is just an idle rumor."

Cornelia said, "Will you dissemble and not tell me the truth? Surely you don't do well to frighten me like this: You never look this pale except when you are very angry. I command you, upon my blessing — nay, I'll call the duke, Brachiano, and he shall school you. He shall make you tell me."

Marcello said, "Don't make known a fear, which when revealed would convert to laughter: People will laugh at you if you tell them what you are afraid will happen. What you fear is not so."

He saw the crucifix she was wearing around her neck and asked her, "Wasn't this crucifix my father's?"

"Yes, it was," Cornelia replied.

Marcello said, "I have heard you say that while you were giving my brother suck that he took the crucifix between his hands, and broke a limb off."

While Marcello was saying these words, Flamineo entered the room without being seen. He was holding Marcello's sword.

"Yes, but that limb is now mended," Cornelia said.

Flamineo said, "I have brought your weapon back."

He ran Marcello through with the sword.

"Oh!" Cornelia shouted. "Oh, my horror!"

Mortally wounded, Marcello said, "You have brought it home, indeed."

"Help!" Cornelia shouted. "Oh, he's murdered!"

"Do you turn your gall up?" Flamineo said to Marcello. "I'll go to sanctuary and send a surgeon to you."

Flamineo was morbidly mocking Marcello. The gall bladder was regarded as the seat of anger, and Flamineo was pretending to be surprised that Marcello was angry. This society believed that an excess of blood was a cause of an illness that could be cured by bloodletting. Flamineo had just let blood out from Marcello's body, and so Marcello ought to be happy because he was being medically treated.

In this society, a fugitive could go to a church and get sanctuary. As long as they were in the church, they could not be arrested.

Flamineo exited just before Hortensio, Carlo, and Pedro arrived.

"What!" Hortensio said, "Lying wounded on the ground!"

Marcello said, "Oh, mother, now remember what I said about the breaking of the crucifix! Farewell.

"There are some sins that heaven duly punishes in a whole family. This is what it is to rise by all dishonest means! Let all men know that a tree shall for a long time keep a steady foot if its branches spread no wider than the root."

After saying this proverb against excessive ambition, he died.

"Oh, my perpetual sorrow!" Cornelia said.

"Virtuous Marcello!" Hortensio said. "He's dead. Please leave him, lady. Come, you shall."

Hortensio and Carlo pulled her away from the body of her son.

Cornelia objected, "He is not dead; he's in a trance."

She was wrong.

She continued, "Why, here's nobody who shall get anything by his death. Let me call him again, for God's sake!"

Carlo said, "I wish that you were deceived."

Certainly, Flamineo wanted Marcello dead.

Certainly, Marcello was dead.

Cornelia cried, "Oh, you abuse me! You abuse me! You abuse me! How many have gone away thus, for lack of medical attendance! Lift up his head! Lift up his head! His bleeding inward will kill him."

Hortensio said, "You see that his soul has departed."

Cornelia pleaded, "Let me come to him; give him to me as he is, if he has turned to earth. Let me but give him one hearty kiss, and you shall put us both in one coffin. Fetch a looking-glass: See if his breath will not stain it. Or pull out some feathers from my pillow, and lay them on his lips to see if he is breathing. Will you lose him for a little painstaking?"

Hortensio said, "Your kindest duty is to pray for him."

Cornelia said, "I would not pray for him yet. He may live to lay me in the ground and pray for me, if you'll let me come to him."

Brachiano, completely armed, arrived with Flamineo and others, including the disguised Lodovico and the disguised Francisco de Medici. Some attendants were among those present.

Brachiano detached the beaver — the lower part of his helmet — set it aside, and asked Flamineo about the murder, "Was this your handiwork?"

Flamineo replied, "It was my misfortune."

Cornelia said, "He lies! He lies! He did not kill him: These men have killed him — they would not let him be better looked after."

Brachiano said, "Have comfort, my grieved mother-in-law."

Cornelia replied, "Oh, you screech-owl!"

His existence made her angry. He was alive, while her son was not.

This society regarded screech-owls as birds of ill omen.

Hortensio said, "Don't be like that, good madam."

Cornelia cried, "Let me go! Let me go!"

She ran to Flamineo with her knife drawn, but coming to him, she let her knife fall.

She said, "May the God of heaven forgive thee! Don't you wonder why I pray for thee? I'll tell thee what's the reason: I have scarcely enough breath and life left to number twenty minutes. I'd rather not spend that in cursing. Fare thee well. Half of thyself lies there" — she pointed to Marcello's corpse — "and may thou live to fill an hourglass with his moldered, decayed-to-dust ashes to tell that thou should spend the time to come in blessed repentance!"

Brachiano said, "Mother-in-law, please tell me how he came by his death? What was the quarrel?"

Cornelia had lost one son; she did not want to lose her other son, so she lied to Brachiano and put the blame for the fight on Marcello.

Cornelia said, "Indeed, Marcello — my younger boy — presumed too much upon his manhood, gave Flamineo bitter words, drew his sword first, and so, I don't know how, for I was out of my wits, he fell with his head just in my bosom."

The page, who was an eyewitness, said quietly, "That is not true, madam."

Cornelia said quietly to the page, "I pray to thee, be quiet. One arrow's lost already; it would be vain to lose this arrow, for that first arrow will never be found again."

When an arrow was lost, the archer would sometimes shoot a second arrow in the same direction and at the same velocity in an attempt to find the first arrow.

Brachiano ordered some attendants, "Go, bear the body to Cornelia's lodging. And we command that no one acquaint our duchess with this sad incident."

This was his and her wedding day; he did not want her to mourn yet.

He then said, "As for you, Flamineo, listen — I will not grant your pardon."

"No?" Flamineo asked.

Brachiano said, "I will grant you only a lease of your life; and that shall last for only one day. Thou shall be forced each evening to renew it, or be hanged."

Every evening, Flamineo would have to humbly ask Brachiano to allow him to live for another day.

Flamineo replied, "At your pleasure."

While everyone was distracted, the disguised Lodovico sprinkled Brachiano's beaver with a poison.

The beaver is the lower part of a helmet; it is detachable.

Flamineo said to Brachiano, "Your will is law now, and I'll not meddle with it."

Brachiano said, "You once did defy me in your sister's lodging: I'll now keep you in awe for it."

He was referring to the time that he had ordered Flamineo to get Vittoria, who was then in the House of Convertites.

Using the majestic plural, Brachiano looked around and asked, "Where's our beaver?"

The disguised Francisco de Medici said quietly to himself, "He calls for his destruction."

He then said out loud, pretending to be sad about Marcello's death, "Noble youth, I pity thy sad fate!"

He then said quietly to himself, "Now to the barriers."

He was looking forward to seeing that entertainment. Brachiano would put on his beaver there so he could participate.

The disguised Francisco de Medici then continued saying quietly to himself, "This shall further his passage to the black lake in hell: The last good deed Brachiano did, he pardoned murder."

People fought at barriers. First one man fought against another man, and then a team of three men fought against another team of three men.

Brachiano, Flamineo, Vittoria, young Giovanni, the disguised Francisco de Medici, the six ambassadors, guards, and attendants were present.

Suddenly ill, Brachiano called, "An armorer! By God's death, an armorer!"

"Armorer!" Flamineo shouted. "Where's the armorer?"

Brachiano ordered, "Tear off my beaver."

"Are you hurt, my lord?" Flamineo asked.

"Oh, my brain's on fire!" Brachiano answered.

The armorer arrived.

"The helmet is poisoned," Brachiano said.

The armorer began to plead, "My lord, upon my soul —"

Brachiano ordered, "Take him away to be tortured."

The guard led the armorer away.

Brachiano continued, "There are some great ones — some powerful men — who have a hand in this, and they are close around me."

Vittoria said, "Oh, my loved lord! Poisoned!"

Flamineo ordered, "Remove the barriers."

He added, "Here's unfortunate revels!"

Then he ordered, "Call the physicians."

Two physicians arrived.

"A plague upon you!" Flamineo cursed. "We have too much of your cunning here already: I fear the ambassadors are likewise poisoned."

"Oh, I am gone already!" Brachiano said. "The infection flies to my brain and heart. Oh, thou strong heart! There's such a covenant between the world and it — they're loath to break it."

"Oh, my most loved father!" young Giovanni, Brachiano's son, said.

"Take the boy away," Brachiano ordered.

He did not want his son to see him die.

Another guard led away young Giovanni.

Brachiano asked about his newly wedded wife, Vittoria, "Where's this good woman?"

Seeing her, he said, "Had I infinite worlds, they would be too little for thee. Must I leave thee?"

He asked the physicians, "What do you say, screech-owls? Is the venom mortal?"

Screech-owls were birds of ill omen.

A physician said, "It is most deadly."

Brachiano replied, "Most corrupted politic hangman, you kill without book; but your art to save fails you as often as great men's needy friends."

Physicians have no problem when it comes to killing people: they don't need to consult a medical book to do that. Where physicians have a problem is healing people.

A great man's needy friends are talented at asking for help; they lack talent when it comes to giving help.

Brachiano continued, "I who have given life to offending slaves and wretched murderers, haven't I the power to lengthen my own life a twelvemonth?"

He said to Vittoria, "Do not kiss me, for the kiss shall poison thee. The poison that shall kill me shall also then kill you. This unction has been sent from the great Duke of Florence."

"Unction" can mean extreme unction: the last rites that are given to someone who is expected to die.

"Unction" can also mean rubbing with oil. His beaver had been rubbed with poison.

Brachiano knew who must be behind his death.

The disguised Francisco de Medici said, "Sir, be of comfort."

Brachiano said, "Oh, thou soft natural death, which is joint-twin to sweetest slumber!"

A proverb stated, "Sleep is the brother of death."

He continued, "No rough-bearded — long-tailed — comet stares on thy mild departure; the dull owl beats not against thy casement; the hoarse wolf scents not thy carrion: pity waits on and wraps thy corpse in a shroud, while horror waits on princes' corpses."

Princes often die violently; not being a prince increases one's chances of dying a natural death.

Mourning, Vittoria said, "I am lost forever."

Brachiano said, "How miserable a thing it is to die among women howling!"

Lodovico and Gasparo, disguised as Capuchins, arrived.

Brachiano asked, "Who are those men?"

Flamineo replied, "Franciscans. They have brought the extreme unction."

The Capuchins were an offshoot of the Franciscans. In addition, Lodovico and Gasparo were Franciscans in the sense of being in the faction of Francisco de Medici.

Brachiano ordered, "On pain of death, let no man name death to me: It is a word infinitely terrible.

"Withdraw into our private apartment."

Everyone except the disguised Francisco de Medici and Flamineo exited.

Flamineo said, "To see what solitariness surrounds dying princes!

"As heretofore they have unpeopled towns, divorced friends, and made great houses inhospitable, so now — oh, justice! — where are their flatterers now? Flatterers are only the shadows of princes' bodies; the least thick cloud makes them invisible.

The disguised Francisco de Medici said, "There's great moan made for him."

Many were mourning Brachiano's poisoning.

Flamineo said, "Indeed, for some few hours salt-water tears will run most plentifully in every office of the court; but, believe it, most of them weep over their stepmothers' graves."

The stereotype of stepmothers in this society was that they were cruel to their stepchildren, and so tears shed by their stepchildren over the stepmother's grave would be hypocritical.

The disguised Francisco de Medici asked, "What do you mean?"

Flamineo said, "Why, they dissemble; as some men do who live within the compass of the verge."

The verge was the area within twelve miles of a royal court. People living that close would be sure to maintain an appearance of mourning whether or not they truly mourned.

The disguised Francisco de Medici said, "Come, you have thrived well under him."

Flamineo said, "Indeed, like a wolf in a woman's breast, I have been fed with poultry."

A wolf was an ulcer — a cancer — that devoured the ill person's flesh. In this society, physicians would daily place chicken or other meat over the ulcer, supposing that the ulcer would feed on the chicken or other meat rather than the ill person's flesh.

When saying "poultry," Flamineo may have been punning on the word "paltry."

He continued, "But as for money, understand me, I had as good a will to cheat him as ever an officer of them all, but I lacked enough cunning to do it."

"What did thou think of him?" the disguised Francisco de Medici asked. "Indeed, speak freely."

Flamineo replied, "He was a kind of statesman, of the kind who would sooner have reckoned how many cannon-bullets he had discharged against a town in order to count his expense that way, rather than think how many of his valiant and deserving subjects he had lost before the town."

"Oh, speak well of the duke!" the disguised Francisco de Medici said.

Most likely, he had done the same thing that Flamineo had accused Brachiano of doing.

Flamineo said, "I have finished."

Lodovico, still disguised as a Capuchin, entered the scene.

He asked, "Will thou hear some of my court-wisdom? To reprehend princes is dangerous, and to over-commend some of them is palpable lying."

"How is it with the duke?" the disguised Francisco de Medici asked.

"He is most deadly ill," the disguised Lodovico said. "He's fallen into a strange distraction: He talks of battles and monopolies, the levying of taxes; and from that descends to the most brainsick language. His mind fastens on twenty several objects, which confound deep sense with folly.

"Such a fearful end may teach some men who bear too lofty a crest that although they live the happiest of lives yet they don't die the best death.

"He has conferred the whole state of the dukedom upon your sister, Vittoria, until the prince Giovanni arrives at the age of maturity."

Flamineo said, "There's some good luck in that yet."

As they talked, they walked over to Brachiano's private apartment.

The disguised Francisco de Medici said, "Look, he is in sight."

Brachiano was in a bed, surrounded by Vittoria and others.

As they walked over to him, the disguised Francisco de Medici said quietly to Flamineo and the disguised Lodovico, "There's death in his face already."

Vittoria said, "Oh, my good lord!"

Brachiano was ill, and he jumped from topic to topic and sometimes imagined he was talking to people who were not present.

First, he imagined that he was talking to a disgraced steward.

Brachiano said, "Go away, you have abused me. You have conveyed money from out of our territories, bought and sold offices, oppressed the poor, and I never dreamt that would happen. Make up your accounts. From now on I'll be my own steward."

In this society, taking money out of the country was a serious offence.

Flamineo said, "Sir, have patience."

Brachiano then felt that he was guilty, too:

"Indeed, I am to blame and too blameworthy. For did you ever hear the dusky raven chide blackness? Or was it ever known for the devil to rail against cloven creatures?"

Brachiano had not complained against or taken action to stop the actions of the steward and so he shared the steward's guilt.

Vittoria said, "Oh, my lord!"

Brachiano then imagined that he was going to have a meal.

He said, "Let me have some quails to supper."

"Sir, you shall," Flamineo said.

Brachiano changed his mind: "No, some fried dog-fish; your quails feed on poison."

Quails were a delicacy; this society wrongly believed that they fed on poison. Dog-fish were not a delicacy.

Prostitutes were sometimes called quails; calling someone a dog-fish was a grave insult.

Brachiano said, "That old dog-fox, that politician, the Duke of Florence! I'll forswear hunting, and turn dog-killer."

In this society, people were hired to kill dangerous stray dogs and rabid dogs.

Brachiano continued, "Splendid! I'll be friends with him; for, listen carefully, sir, one dog always sets another a-barking. Peace, peace!"

He then imagined he was seeing a visitor.

He said, "Yonder's a fine slave come in now."

"Where?" Flamineo asked.

"Why, there," Brachiano said. "In a blue cap, and a pair of breeches with a large codpiece: Ha! Ha! Ha! Look, his codpiece is stuck full of pins, with pearls on the head of them."

A codpiece was a pouch that covered a man's genitals. They could be decorated with pins.

Brachiano asked, "Don't you know who he is?"

"No, my lord," Flamineo replied.

Brachiano said, "Why, it's the devil. I know him by a great rose he wears on his shoe, to hide his cloven foot."

A fashion of the time was to wear large rosettes on one's shoes.

Brachiano continued, "I'll debate with him; he's a rare linguist."

The devil was skilled at rhetoric; the devil also knew every language.

Vittoria said, "My lord, here's nothing."

Brachiano said, "Nothing! Rare! Nothing! When I want money, our treasury is empty, there is nothing. I'll not be treated this way."

Vittoria said, "Oh, lie still, my lord!"

Brachiano said, "Look! Look! Flamineo, who killed his brother, is dancing on the tightropes there, and he carries a moneybag in each hand to keep him even, for fear of breaking his neck.

"And there's a lawyer in a garment trimmed with velvet, who stares with an open mouth as he watches for when the money will fall.

"How the rogue Brachiano cuts capers! The rogue should have been in a halter."

A halter is a noose.

Brachiano then said, "There! Who's she?"

"Vittoria, my lord," Flamineo said.

Brachiano said, "Ha! Ha! Ha! Her hair is sprinkled with iris-root powder, which makes her look as if she had sinned in the pastry."

In preparation for her wedding, Vittoria's hair had been sprinkled with perfumed iris-root powder, which lightened its color. Brachiano was saying that the iris-root powder looked like flour, which Vittoria could have gotten in her hair if she had been having sex in the pantry.

Brachiano then asked, "Who's he?"

Flamineo replied, "A divine, my lord."

Lodovico and Gasparo, both disguised and wearing the clothing of Capuchins, were both present.

Brachiano said, "He will be drunk; avoid him. The argument is fearful, when churchmen stagger in it."

"Argument" can mean 1) defense (based on logic and reason) of a position in a debate, 2) the topic of a debate, and/or 3) the debate itself.

Churchmen can stagger because 1) they are drunk, or 2) someone has struck them hard.

Brachiano then said, "Look, six grey rats that have lost their tails crawl upon the pillow; send for a rat-catcher."

Witches were supposed to be able to take the shape of an animal, but the witch-animals would be tail-less.

He then said, "I'll do a miracle — I'll free the court from all foul vermin."

He may have been thinking of the Pied Piper of Hamelin.

Brachiano then asked, "Where's Flamineo?"

Flamineo said, "I do not like that he names me so often, especially on his deathbed; it is a sign I shall not live long. See, he's near his end."

Lodovico and Gasparo brought a crucifix and hallowed — consecrated — candle to his bed.

The disguised Lodovico said, "Please, give us permission to do what needs to be done."

He then said in Latin, "*Attende, domine Brachiane.*"

["Listen, Lord Brachiano."]

Flamineo said, "See how firmly he fixes his eye upon the crucifix."

Vittoria said, "Oh, hold it steady! It settles his wild spirits, and so his eyes melt into tears."

The disguised Lodovico and the disguised Gasparo spoke to the dying Brachiano in Latin.

Holding the crucifix, the disguised Lodovico said, "*Domine Brachiane, solebas in bello tutus esse tuo clypeo; nunc hunc clypeum hosti tuo opponas infernali.*"

["Lord Brachiano, you used to be guarded in battle by your shield; now you will use this shield — the crucifix — to oppose your infernal enemy."]

Holding the consecrated candle, the disguised Gasparo said, "*Olim hastâ valuisti in bello; nunc hanc sacram hastam vibrabis contra hostem animarum.*"

["In former times you prevailed with a spear in the battle; now you will use this sacred spear — the consecrated candle — against the enemy of souls."]

Brachiano had now lost the power of speech, and so the "Capuchin monks" began to ask him to move his head to indicate his assent to what they were asking him to approve.

The disguised Lodovico said, "*Attende, Domine Brachiane, si nunc quoque probes ea, quae acta sunt inter nos, flecte caput in dextrum.*"

["Listen, Lord Brachiano, if now you also approve of the things that were done between us, turn your head to the right."]

The disguised Gasparo said, "*Esto securus, Domine Brachiane; cogita, quantum habeas meritorum; denique memineris mean animam pro tuâ oppignoratum si quid esset periculi.*"

["Be assured, Lord Brachiano; think about how many good deeds you have done; lastly, remember that my soul is pledged to yours, if there is any danger."]

The disguised Lodovico said, "*Si nunc quoque probas ea, quae acta sunt inter nos, flecte caput in loevum.*"

["If now you also approve of the things that were done between us, turn your head to the left."]

The disguised Lodovico said, "He is departing. Please, everyone stand outside, and let us only whisper in his ears some private meditations, which our order does not permit you to hear."

Everyone except the dying Brachiano and the disguised Lodovico and the disguised Gasparo exited.

Lodovico and Gasparo briefly removed enough of their disguises to reveal to Brachiano who they were, and then they disguised themselves again.

"Brachiano," Gasparo said.

"Devil Brachiano, thou are damned," Lodovico said.

"Perpetually," Gasparo said.

"A slave condemned and given up to the gallows is thy great lord and master," Lodovico said.

"True; for thou are given up to the devil," Gasparo said.

In the book of Esther, the evil Haman built a gallows to hang the good Mordecai, but Haman ended up swinging from the gallows. Sometimes, God allows an evil being to appear to be victorious but then God suddenly achieves victory.

Or possibly, Lodovico meant that Brachiano was a follower of the bad thief who did not repent when he was crucified alongside Jesus. In this society, a gallows can be a cross.

Or possibly, Lodovico and Gasparo were using "gallows" to mean punishment in general — and in particular the punishment suffered by the devil and damned souls in hell.

"Oh, you slave!" Lodovico said. "You who were held to be the famous politician, whose art was poison —"

Gasparo said, "— and whose conscience was murder —"

Lodovico said, "— who would have broken your wife's neck by throwing her down the stairs, before she was poisoned —"

Gasparo said, "— who had your villainous salads —"

Salads can be poisoned.

Lodovico said, "— and fine decorated bottles, and perfumes, equally deadly to a winter plague."

Perfumes in fine decorated bottles can be poisonous.

The plague tended to be most virulent during the summer and died out during the winter, so a winter's plague was especially virulent.

Gasparo and Lodovico began to name poisons.

Gasparo said, "Now there's mercury —"

Lodovico said, "— and copperas —"

Gasparo said, "— and quicksilver —"

Lodovico said, "— with other devilish apothecary stuff, a-melting in your politic — maliciously cunning — brains. Do thou hear?"

Pointing to Lodovico, Gasparo said, "This is Count Lodovico."

Pointing to Gasparo, Lodovico said, "And this is Gasparo."

He then said, "And thou shall die like a poor rogue —"

Gasparo said, "— and stink like a dead fly-blown dog —"

Lodovico said, "— and be forgotten before the funeral sermon."

Recovering his voice, Brachiano shouted, "Vittoria! Vittoria!"

Lodovico said, "Oh, the cursed devil comes to himself again! We are ruined."

Gasparo said, "Strangle him in private."

He went to the door and met Vittoria and the attendants as they tried to enter the room.

Lodovico, his body hiding what he was doing from the others, was strangling Brachiano and preventing him from calling out.

Brachiano was too weak to fight back.

Gasparo said to Vittoria and the attendants, "What? Will you call him again to live in treble torments? For charity, for Christian charity, leave the chamber."

Vittoria and the attendants exited.

Lodovico said quietly to Brachiano, "You would prate, sir? This is a true-love knot sent from the Duke of Florence."

He strangled Brachiano with a rosary made of chain.

Gasparo asked quietly, "Is it done?"

"The snuff is out," Lodovico said quietly. "No woman-keeper — nurse — in the world, even if she had practiced for seven years at the pestilence-hospital, could have done it more skillfully."

Nurses were sometimes accused of killing their patients.

The disguised Lodovico went to the door and said, "My lords, he's dead."

Vittoria and the attendants entered, along with the disguised Francisco de Medici and Flamineo.

All said, "Rest to his soul!"

Vittoria said, "Oh, me! This place is hell."

Everyone exited except the disguised Francisco de Medici, Flamineo, and the disguised Lodovico.

The disguised Francisco de Medici said, "How heavily she takes it!"

"Oh, yes, yes," Flamineo said. "If women had navigable rivers in their eyes, they would dispend all their water as tears. Surely, I wonder why we should wish more rivers to come to the city, when women sell water so good cheap.

"I'll tell thee that these are only Moorish shades of griefs or fears. There's nothing sooner dry than women's tears.

"Why, here's an end of all my harvest; Brachiano has given me nothing. Court promises! Let wise men count themselves accursed, for while you live, he who scores best, pays worst."

In other words: He who runs up the largest debt ends up paying the least for it.

Sometimes, people skip on the debt. Sometimes, people avoid paying the debt because they die.

According to Flamineo, Brachiano had promised him much but delivered on none of the promises.

The disguised Francisco de Medici — the Duke of Florence — said, "Surely, this was the Duke of Florence's doing."

"Very likely," Flamineo said. "Those are found to be weighty strokes that come from the hand, but those are killing strokes that come from the head."

Francisco de Medici used his head to punish his enemies.

Flamineo continued, "Oh, the splendid tricks of a Machiavellian! He does not come like a gross plodding slave and beat you to death; no, my ingenious knave, he tickles you to death and makes you die laughing, as if you had swallowed down a pound of saffron."

This culture believed that a little saffron would make a man merry, but too much saffron would make a man dead.

Flamineo continued:

"You see the feat; it is practiced in a trice.

"To teach court honesty that it jumps on ice."

In other words: Honest men at court are on slippery ice — in danger — because of the schemers around them.

Or perhaps Flamineo said, "To teach 'court honesty' that it jumps on ice."

In other words: Dishonest men at court are on slippery ice — in danger — because of the schemers around them.

The disguised Francisco de Medici said, "Now the people have liberty to talk about and comment on his vices."

Flamineo said, "Misery of princes, who must necessarily be censured by their inferiors! They are not only blamed for doing things that are ill, but for not doing all that all men want them to do. One would be better off being a thresher.

"By God's death! I would like to speak with this duke yet."

Which duke? The Duke of Brachiano? Or the Duke of Florence?

The disguised Francisco de Medici asked, "Now he's dead?"

Flamineo said, "I cannot conjure and bring him here; but if prayers or oaths will get to the speech of him, then even though forty devils attend on him in his livery of flames, I'll speak to him, and shake him by the hand, although I be blasted."

In this society, the word "speech" can mean "conversation."

If he was talking about the Duke of Brachiano, he might want to shake his hand to see if there was a way he might gain something from him.

If he was talking about the Duke of Florence, he might want to shake his hand because he had killed Brachiano.

Due to having committed murder, the Duke of Florence might have a metaphorical livery of flames now and a literal livery of flames later.

Flamineo exited.

Francisco de Medici said, "Excellent Lodovico! Did you terrify him at the last gasp?"

"Yes," Lodovico said, "and so idly that the duke almost terrified us."

They had easily terrified Brachiano, and the Duke of Brachiano was so terrified that they were almost terrified by his terror.

Francisco de Medici asked, "How?"

Zanche, Vittoria's Moorish maid, entered the room.

Seeing her, Lodovico said, "You shall hear that hereafter.

"Look, yonder's the infernal spirit of darkness, who would have some fun.

"Now to the revelation of that secret she promised when she fell in love with you."

Francisco de Medici, who was disguised as a Moor, said to Zanche, who was a Moor, "You're passionately met in this sad world."

"I would have you look up, sir," Zanche said. "These court tears don't claim your tribute to them. You have no reason to pretend to mourn. Let those who guiltily partake in the sad cause weep.

"I knew last night, by a sad dream I had, that some mischief would ensue, yet, to say the truth, my dream mostly concerned you."

The disguised Lodovico whispered to Francisco de Medici, "Shall we fall to dreaming?"

The disguised Francisco de Medici whispered back, "Yes, and for the sake of appearances I'll dream with her."

Zanche said, "I thought, sir, that you came stealing to my bed."

The disguised Francisco de Medici said, "Will thou believe me, sweetheart? By this light, I swear that I was dreaming about thee, too, for I thought I saw thee naked."

Zanche said, "For shame, sir! As I told you, I thought you lay down by me."

Francisco de Medici said, "So dreamt I, and lest thou should take cold, I covered thee with this Irish mantle."

Poor rural Irish often wore a mantle — a kind of blanket — as their only garment; underneath it they were naked.

Zanche said, "Truly I did dream that you were somewhat bold with me: but to come to it —"

The disguised Lodovico said, "What! What! I hope you will not go to it here."

"Go to it" can mean "have sex."

The disguised Francisco de Medici said, "Nay, you must hear my dream out."

"Well, sir, continue relating your dream," Zanche said.

The disguised Francisco de Medici said, "When I threw the mantle over thee, you laughed exceedingly, I thought."

"Laugh!" Zanche said.

The disguised Francisco de Medici said, "And you cried out that the hair tickled thee."

Pubic hair could sexually tickle her.

"There was a dream indeed!" Zanche said.

The disguised Lodovico whispered to Francisco de Medici, "Listen to her, I beg thee. She simpers like the suds a collier has been washed in."

In this society, the word "simper" had the meaning "simmer" as well as its usual meaning.

Using its usual meaning, Zanche was simpering with delight at hearing the disguised Francisco de Medici's bawdy talk.

Using the meaning of "simmer," Zanche was heating up with sexual desire at hearing the disguised Francisco de Medici's bawdy talk.

A collier is a seller of coal; as such, he would be dirty, and the suds he bathed in would become dirty — black, like Zanche.

Simmering liquids can form suds.

Zanche said to the disguised Francisco de Medici, "Come, sir; good fortune attends you. I did tell you that I would reveal a secret.

"Isabella, the Duke of Florence's sister, was poisoned by a perfumed picture, and Camillo's neck was broken by damned Flamineo — the blame for Camillo's 'accident' was laid on a vaulting-horse."

"Most strange!" the disguised Francisco de Medici said.

"Most true," Zanche said.

The disguised Lodovico said, "The bed of snakes is broken."

These days, we would say "the nest of snakes."

Zanche said, "I sadly confess that I had a hand in the black deed."

The disguised Francisco de Medici guessed, "Thou kept their counsel secret."

She had not told anyone about the plot.

"Right," Zanche said. "For which, urged by contrition, I intend to rob Vittoria this night."

The disguised Lodovico said, "Excellent penitence! Usurers dream about it while they sleep out sermons."

The usurers were Jews who were required to attend Christian sermons. According to Lodovico, they slept during the sermons.

Zanche said, "To further our escape, I have entreated permission to retire until the funeral to a friend in the country. That excuse will further our escape. In coin and jewels, I shall at least make good for your use a hundred thousand crowns."

"Oh, noble wench!" the disguised Francisco de Medici said.

Lodovico thought, *Those crowns we'll share.*

Zanche said, "It is a dowry, I think, that should make that sun-burnt proverb false, and wash the Ethiopian white."

Jeremiah 13:23 states, "*Can the Ethiopian change his skin, or the leopard his spots? Then may ye also do good, that are accustomed to do evil*" (King James Version).

"It shall," the disguised Francisco de Medici said. "Go and do what needs to be done."

Zanche said, "Be ready for our flight."

The disguised Francisco de Medici said, "An hour before day."

Zanche exited.

He said to Lodovico, "Oh, strange discovery! Why, until now we didn't know the circumstances of the deaths of Isabella and Camillo: my sister and Vittoria's husband."

Zanche returned and asked the disguised Francisco de Medici, "You'll wait about midnight in the chapel?"

The disguised Francisco de Medici said, "Yes, I will wait there."

Zanche exited.

Lodovico said, "Why, now our action's justified."

They had reasons to justify the murder of Brachiano and the theft of valuables from Vittoria.

Francisco de Medici said, "Tush for justice! Who cares about justice? What justice harms what we want to do?

"We now, like the partridge, purge the disease with laurel; for the fame shall crown the enterprise, and acquit the shame."

Partridges were thought to eat laurel as a purgative.

The laurel wreath is a symbol of victory, and Francisco de Medici was saying that the victory they would achieve would overpower the taint of the shameful means they used to achieve the victory.

— 5.4 —

Flamineo and the disguised Gasparo stood together in a room. Young Giovanni, accompanied by some attendants, entered the room.

The disguised Gasparo whispered, "There's the young duke."

Now that his father was dead, young Giovanni was duke.

The disguised Gasparo then whispered, "Did you ever see a sweeter prince?"

Flamineo whispered, "I have known a poor woman's bastard better favored — more handsome. This is something I say behind his back. Now, when it comes to saying something to his face — all comparisons were hateful."

All comparisons would be hateful because, according to Flamineo, young Giovanni was ugly. Flamineo could bring himself to flatter young Giovanni, but Flamineo would hate doing it.

Flamineo then whispered, "Wise was the courtly peacock that, being a great minion, and being compared for beauty by some dottrels — foolish birds — that stood nearby the kingly eagle, said the eagle was a far fairer bird than herself, not in respect of her feathers, but in respect of her long talons: Young Giovanni's will grow out in time."

Young Giovanni might be called handsome, but it would be because of his power. He could order to be killed anyone who displeased him.

Young Giovanni and his attendants walked over to Flamineo and the disguised Gasparo.

Flamineo said, "My gracious lord."

Young Giovanni said, "I tell you to leave me, sir."

He meant that he did not want Flamineo in his court, although Flamineo was his step-mother's brother.

"Your grace must be merry and joking," Flamineo replied. "It is I who have cause to mourn; for you know what the little boy who rode behind his father on horseback said?"

Young Giovanni asked, "Why, what did he say?"

Flamineo answered, "'When you are dead, father,' said he, 'I hope that I shall ride in the saddle.'

"Oh, it is a brave thing for a man to sit by himself! He may stretch himself in the stirrups, look about, and see the whole compass of the hemisphere. You're now, my lord, in the saddle."

Young Giovanni said, "Study your prayers, sir, and be penitent. It would be fitting for you to think about what has formerly been. I have heard grief called the eldest child of sin."

Flamineo needed to think about his sins and repent. Part of repentance is feeling grief at having sinned.

Young Giovanni and his attendants — and Gasparo — exited. Flamineo was alone.

"Study my prayers!" Flamineo said to himself. "He threatens me divinely! I am falling to pieces already. I don't care, though, even if like Anacharsis, I were pounded to death in a mortar: and yet that death were fitter for usurers' gold and themselves to be beaten together, to make a most cordial cullis for the devil."

Instead of Anacharsis, who was a Thracian prince, Flamineo meant Anaxarchus, who was pounded to death in a mortar with iron pestles because he had insulted the tyrant Nicocreon of Cyprus.

Flamineo believed that usurers and their gold ought to be pounded in a mortar to make a fortifying broth for the devil.

Flamineo added, "Young Giovanni has his uncle's villainous look already, in decimo-sexto."

Decimo-sexto is a small-sized book. Its pages are one-sixteenth of a full sheet of paper.

A courtier entered the room.

Flamineo asked, "Now, sir, who are you?"

The courtier said, "It is the pleasure, sir, of the young duke, that you stay away from the presence-room, and all rooms that owe him reverence."

In other words: Stay away from young Giovanni.

Flamineo replied, "So the wolf and the raven are very pretty fools when they are young."

When they are older, they become more dangerous.

The wolf is a predator, and the raven is a bird of ill omen.

When young Giovanni became an adult, he would be dangerous.

Flamineo asked, "It is your duty, sir, to keep me out?"

"So the duke wills," the courtier replied.

Flamineo said, "Verily, Master Courtier, extremity is not to be used in all duties.

"Let's say that a gentlewoman were taken out of her bed about midnight, and committed to Castle Angelo, to the tower yonder, with nothing about her but her smock. Would it not show a cruel part in the gentleman-porter to lay claim to her upper garment, pull it over her head and ears, and put her in the prison naked?"

The courtier said, "Very good. You are merry. You make jokes."

He exited.

Flamineo said to himself, "Does he make a court-ejectment of me? Does he banish me from the court? A flaming firebrand casts more smoke outside a chimney than within it. I'll smother some of them."

He was punning on his name and threatening to be more dangerous outside the court than within it.

The disguised Francisco de Medici entered the room.

"What is the news now?" Flamineo asked, "Thou are sad."

The disguised Francisco de Medici replied, "I just now saw the most piteous sight."

Flamineo said, "Thou see another pitiful sight here: a pitiful degraded courtier."

He was referring to himself.

The disguised Francisco de Medici said, "Your reverend mother has become a very old woman in the past two hours.

"I found them putting the shroud on Marcello's corpse, and there is such a solemn melody of doleful songs, tears, and sad elegies, such as old granddames, watching by the dead, were accustomed to outwear the nights with, that, believe me, I had no eyes to guide me from the room — my eyes were blinded by tears."

Flamineo said, "I will see them."

The disguised Francisco de Medici said, "It would not be charitable for you to see them; for their seeing you will add to their tears."

By this time, everyone knew that Flamineo had murdered his brother, Marcello.

"I will see them," Flamineo said. "They are behind the traverse; I'll reveal their superstitious howling."

They were in a nearby room, behind a partition.

Flamineo moved the partition, revealing Cornelia, Zanche the Moor, and three other ladies preparing Marcello's corpse while singing a sad song.

Cornelia, the mother of Marcello, Flamineo, and Vittoria, was aged by grief.

After the song was sung, Cornelia said, "This rosemary is withered; please, get fresh rosemary."

Rosemary symbolizes love, death, and remembrance.

Cornelia continued, "I would have these herbs grow upon his grave, when I am dead and rotten.

"Hand me the bay leaves. I'll tie a garland here about his head."

A garland or wreath made of bay leaves — also known as laurel leaves — symbolizes triumph and victory. In Christianity, bay leaves symbolize the resurrection of Christ.

She continued, "I have kept this shroud for the past twenty years, and every day I have hallowed it with my prayers; I did not think he would have wore it."

The shroud had been intended for her own use.

Zanche said, "Look, who are yonder?"

Cornelia said, "Oh, hand me the flowers!"

Zanche said, "Her ladyship's foolish. She's out of her mind with grief."

One of the women said, "Alas, her grief has turned her into a child again!"

Cornelia said, "You're very welcome."

She then said to Flamineo, "There's rosemary for you, and rue for you, and heart's-ease for you. Please make much use of it; I have more left for myself."

Rue symbolizes sorrow and regret.

Heart's-ease are wild pansies.

The disguised Francisco de Medici pointed to Flamineo and asked Cornelia, "Lady, who is this?"

Cornelia looked at Flamineo, her son, and said, "You are, I take it, the grave-maker."

A grave-maker is a grave-digger. In a way, Flamineo was a grave-maker because he was a murderer.

Recognizing that his mother was mentally disturbed, Flamineo said, "So."

Zanche said, "It is Flamineo."

Cornelia held and looked at Flamineo's hand and replied, "Will you make me such a fool? Here's a white hand. Can blood so soon be washed out?"

Anyone looking at and listening to Cornelia could tell that she was mentally disturbed.

She continued, "Let me see. When screech-owls croak upon the chimney-tops, and the eerie cricket in the oven sings and hops, when yellow spots on your hands appear, be certain then you shall hear about a corpse."

The screech-owl, cricket, and yellow spots were omens of a soon-to-occur death.

Looking at Flamineo's hand, Cornelia said, "Damn, look how speckled it is! He has surely handled a toad."

Toads, which this culture thought were poisonous, had speckled bellies.

Cornelia continued, "Cowslip water is good for the memory. Please, buy me three ounces of it."

Flamineo said, "I wish I were away from here."

"Do you hear, sir?" Cornelia said. "I'll give you a saying that my grandmother was accustomed, when she heard the bell toll, to sing while accompanied by her lute."

Flamineo replied, "Do so, if you want to, do it."

Cornelia sang:

"Call for the robin redbreast, and the wren,

"Since over shady groves they hover,

"And with leaves and flowers do cover

"The friendless bodies of unburied men."

Robins and wrens, which this culture considered to be female robins, were thought to cover the faces and bodies of untended dead human beings.

A proverb stated, "The robin and the wren are God's cock and hen."

Cornelia sang:

"Call unto his funeral dole [rites]

"The ant, the field mouse, and the mole,

"To rear him hillocks that shall keep him warm,

"And (when gay tombs are robbed) sustain no harm;

"But keep the wolf far thence, that's foe to men,

"For with his nails [claws] he'll dig them up again."

In this society, wolves were thought to dig up the corpses of murder victims, not to eat the corpse, but to reveal the murder.

Cornelia sang:

"*They would not bury him 'cause [because] he died in a quarrel;*

"*But I have an answer for them:*

"*Let holy Church receive him duly,*

"*Since he paid the church-tithes truly.*

"*His wealth is summed [counted], and this is all his store,*

"*This poor men get, and great men get no more.*

"*Now the wares are gone, we may shut up shop.*"

Poor men get a grave, and rich men get no more than a grave when they are dead.

Cornelia then said, "Bless you all, good people."

She, Zanche, and the three other ladies exited.

Flamineo said, "I have a strange thing in me, to which I cannot give a name, unless that name is compassion."

He said to the disguised Francisco de Medici, "I ask you to please leave me."

The disguised Francisco de Medici exited.

Alone, Flamineo said to himself, "This night I'll know in detail my fate. I'll be made certain what my rich sister intends to assign me for my service. I have lived riotously ill, like some who live in court, and sometimes when my face was full of smiles, I have felt the maze of conscience in my breast.

"Often gay and honored robes those tortures try."

What is the subject of the sentence? Robes (great men), or tortures?

The sentence can mean 1) Great men experience tortures, or 2) Tortures test great men.

Flamineo continued, "We think caged birds sing, when indeed they cry."

Brachiano's ghost entered the room. He was wearing a leather cassock and breeches, boots, and a cowl, and he was carrying a pot of lily flowers, with a skull in it.

Seeing the ghost, Flamineo said, "Ha! I can stand thee. Come nearer, nearer yet.

"What a mockery has death made thee! Thou look sad.

"In what place are thou? In yonder starry gallery? Or in the cursed dungeon?

"No? Thou will not speak?

"Please, sir, inform me what religion's best for a man to die in?

"Or is it in your knowledge to tell me how long I have to live? That's the most necessary question.

"Thou will not answer?

"Are you silent, like some great men who only walk like shadows up and down, and to no purpose?

"Say to me —"

The ghost of Brachiano threw earth upon him and then showed him the skull.

"What's that?" Flamineo said. "Oh, fatal! He throws earth upon me.

"He shows me a dead man's skull beneath the roots of flowers!

"I ask you to please speak, sir. Our Italian churchmen make us believe that dead men hold conversations with their familiars, and many times will come to bed with them, and eat with them."

The word "familiars" can mean 1) friends, or 2) attendant spirits.

The ghost of Brachiano exited.

"He's gone," Flamineo said, "and see, the skull and earth have vanished. This is beyond melancholy. This is not a hallucination caused by melancholy; it is something more.

"I dare my fate to do its worst.

"Now I will go to my sister's lodging, and sum up all those horrors: the disgrace the prince threw on me, next the piteous sight of my dead brother and my mother's dotage, and last this terrible vision of the ghost of Brachiano."

He drew his sword and said, "All these shall with Vittoria's bounty turn to good, or I will drown this weapon in her blood."

The disguised Francisco de Medici and the disguised Lodovico talked together.

Hortensio came into the room unnoticed, saw the two men talking, hid himself, and eavesdropped on their conversation. Hortensio had served Brachiano as a military officer, and now he served young Giovanni in the same capacity.

The disguised Lodovico said, "My lord, upon my soul you shall go no further and do no more. You have most ridiculously engaged yourself too far already.

"As for my part, I have paid all my debts. That way, if I should chance to fall, my creditors shall not fall with me. I vow to repay and punish all in this bold assembly to the meanest and lowest follower. My lord, leave the city, or I'll forswear the murder."

He meant that unless Francisco de Medici left the city of Padua immediately, he — Lodovico — would not commit the murder that he had sworn to commit.

"Farewell, Lodovico," the disguised Francisco de Medici said. "If thou perish in this glorious act, I'll rear to thy memory that fame which shall in the ashes keep alive thy name."

If Lodovico were to die because of the murder, Francisco de Medici would make sure that he was remembered.

The disguised Lodovico and the disguised Francisco de Medici exited through separate doors.

"There's some black deed on foot," Hortensio said. "I'll immediately go down to the citadel, and raise some forces.

"These strong court-factions that do brook no checks [tolerate no opposition]

"In the career [a short gallop] often break the riders' necks."

Vittoria, attended by Zanche, held a book in her hand. Flamineo walked into the room.

Flamineo said, "What! Are you at your prayers? Give them over. Stop praying."

Vittoria said, "Why, ruffian?"

Flamineo replied, "I come to you about worldly business."

Vittoria stood up, and Flamineo said, "Sit down. Sit down."

Zanche started to leave, but Flamineo restrained her and said, "No, stay, blowze, you may hear it. The doors are secure enough."

A blowse is a fat, red-faced woman. Zanche, of course, was dark-skinned.

Flamineo had locked the doors.

"Ha!" Vittoria said. "Are you drunk?"

Flamineo said, "Yes, yes, with bitter wormwood water; you shall taste some of it soon."

Vittoria asked, "What intends the Fury?"

Furies are female avenging spirits, but Vittoria was calling Flamineo a Fury.

"You are my lord's executrix," Flamineo said, "and I claim reward for my long service."

"For your service!" Vittoria said.

Was murdering their brother service?

Flamineo said, "Come, therefore. Here is pen and ink; set down what you will give me."

Vittoria wrote and said, "There."

"Ha!" Flamineo said. "Have you finished already? It is a very short conveyance."

A conveyance is a document transferring property from one person to another.

Vittoria said, "I will read it out loud:

"*I give that portion to thee, and no other,*

"*Which Cain groaned under, having slain his brother.*"

After Cain killed Abel, his brother, God gave Cain this punishment in Genesis 4:11-12 (King James Version):

11 And now art thou cursed from the earth, which hath opened her mouth to receive thy brother's blood from thy hand;

12 When thou tillest the ground, it shall not henceforth yield unto thee her strength; a fugitive and a vagabond shalt thou be in the earth.

Flamineo said, "A most courtly patent to beg by."

Beggars needed permits to beg, or they could be punished with a whipping.

"You are a villain!" Vittoria said.

Flamineo said, "Has it come to this? They say frights cure agues."

An ague is an illness whose symptoms include fever. An ague is also a state of fear characterized by shaking and shivering.

He continued, "Thou have a devil in thee; I will see if I can scare him from thee."

The two women attempted to leave, but Flamineo told them, "No, sit still."

He then said, "My lord has left me yet two cases of jewels, which shall make me scorn your bounty. You shall see them."

He exited, but he locked the door behind him.

Vittoria said, "Surely he's distracted — he's mentally disturbed."

Zanche said, "Oh, he's desperate!"

"Desperate" meant "without hope." Desperate people committed violent acts, including suicide, which this society believed led to eternal damnation.

Zanche advised Vittoria, "For your own safety, use gentle language when you talk to him."

Flamineo returned with two cases of pistols. Each case contained two pistols.

"Look," he said. "These are better far at a dead lift than all your jewel house."

His sister's jewel could house a penis, and over time, many penises.

Literally, a dead lift occurs when a horse exerts its greatest strength attempting to move a dead weight that it is unable to move. Metaphorically, a dead lift is a sudden emergency.

The word "dead" meant "heavy," but Flamineo was also punning on its usual meaning. A lift can be an erection.

Vittoria said, "And yet, I think, these stones have no fair luster — they are ill set."

The "stones" were the bullets in the pistols. In slang, "stones" can be testicles.

Flamineo said, "I'll turn the right side towards you, so you shall see how they will sparkle."

He pointed the two guns he was holding at her.

"Turn this horror away from me!" Vittoria said. "What do you want? What would you have me do? Is not all that is mine also yours? Have I any children?"

Young Giovanni was her late husband's son.

Flamineo said, "I ask thee, good woman, to not trouble me with this vain worldly business; say your prayers. Neither yourself nor I should outlive him — your late husband — by the numbering of four hours."

Vittoria said, "Did he enjoin it? Did he make this your obligation?"

Flamineo replied, "He did, and it was due to a deadly jealousy, lest any should enjoy thee after him, which urged him to make me vow to do it.

"As for my death, I did propound it voluntarily, knowing that if he could not be safe in his own court, being a great duke, what hope was there then for us?"

Vittoria said, "This is your melancholy, and your despair."

Flamineo said, "Away with such a notion. Thou are a fool to think that politicians are accustomed to kill the effects or injuries and let the cause live. Shall we groan in irons, or be a shameful and a weighty burden to a public scaffold? This is my resolve: I would not live at any man's entreaty, nor die at any man's bidding."

"Will you hear me?" Vittoria asked.

Flamineo said, "My life has done service to other men, but my death shall serve my own turn. Make yourself ready to die."

Vittoria asked, "Do you intend to die indeed?"

Flamineo said, "With as much pleasure as ever my father begat me."

In this society, one meaning of "to die" is "to have an orgasm."

"Are the doors locked?" Vittoria whispered to Zanche.

"Yes, madam," Zanche whispered back.

Vittoria asked Flamineo, "Have you grown to be an atheist? Will you turn your body, which is the splendid palace of the soul, into the soul's slaughter-house?"

Some theologians have believed that the body is the prison of the soul.

She continued, "Oh, the cursed devil, which presents us with all other sins thrice sugared over, presents despair with bitter gall and stibium, yet we carouse — drink — it off."

Stibium is poisonous antimony.

Many sins have an attractive veneer: We can think that committing some sins is "fun." Suicide, however, is always presented as something disagreeable, yet many people willingly commit suicide.

Vittoria whispered to Zanche, "Cry out for help!"

She continued out loud, "Despair makes us forsake that which was made for man — the world — to sink to that which was made for devils — eternal darkness!"

Zanche shouted, "Help! Help!"

Flamineo said, "I'll stop your throat with winter plums."

Plums grow in the summer; winter plums are the dried fruit. In this society, the word "plums" could refer to raisins.

Figuratively, winter plums are bullets.

Vittoria said, "I ask thee to yet remember that millions are now in graves, which on the last day — the Day of Judgment — shall rise shrieking like mandrakes."

Mandrakes were plants that were thought to shriek when pulled from the earth.

Flamineo said, "Stop your prattling, for these are but grammatical laments — they are feminine arguments."

They were laments in words and sounds only; they were not backed up by reason and evidence.

He continued, "And they move me, as some in pulpits move their audiences, more with their exclamations than sense of reason, or sound doctrine."

According to Flamineo, Vittoria's prattling had no sense of reason or sound doctrine. That left exclamations, and Flamineo's manner showed how little those moved him.

Zanche whispered to Vittoria, "Gentle madam, seem to consent, but just persuade him to teach us the way to death. Let him die first."

Vittoria whispered back, "It is a good idea. I understand what you mean."

She then said to Flamineo, "To kill oneself is food that we must take like pills, not chewed, but quickly swallowed. The smart of the wound, or the weakness of the hand, may else bring treble torments."

Killing oneself ought to be done quickly to reduce the pain and suffering of dying. People want to die quickly, not endure a drawn-out, painful death.

Flamineo said, "I have held it to be a wretched and most miserable life that is not able to die."

In other words: A person who is not strong enough to commit suicide leads a wretched and most miserable life.

"Oh, but frailty!" Vittoria said. "Yet I am now resolved; farewell, affliction!"

She then made an apostrophe to her late husband; that is, she addressed her late husband: "Behold, Brachiano, I, who while you lived made a flaming altar of my heart to sacrifice to you, now am ready to sacrifice heart and all."

She then said, "Farewell, Zanche!"

Zanche said, "What, madam! Do you think that I'll outlive you, especially when my best self, Flamineo, goes on the same voyage?"

At one time, she had loved Flamineo.

"Oh, most loved Moor!" Flamineo said.

Zanche said, "Only, by all my love, let me entreat you, since it is most necessary that one of us do violence on ourselves, let you or me be Vittoria's sad taster and teach her how to die."

Kings would not eat until a taster had tasted their food to make sure that it was not poisoned.

Flamineo said, "Thou instruct me nobly; take these pistols because my hand is stained with blood already."

He was saying that he did not want to commit another murder.

He continued, "Two of these you shall level at my breast, the other against your own, and so we'll die most equally contented."

Apparently, he meant that the two women would have two pistols each, one of each pair they would use to shoot him and the other of each pair they would use to shoot each other.

Each of them would avoid committing suicide.

Flamineo added, "But first swear not to outlive me."

Vittoria and Zanche said, "We swear most religiously not to outlive you."

Flamineo said, "Then here's an end of me; farewell, daylight. And, oh, contemptible medicine that takes so long a study, only to preserve so short a life, I take my leave of thee."

He showed them the pistols and said, "These are two cupping-glasses that shall draw all my infected blood out."

In this society, doctors sometimes treated patients by bleeding them. They would heat the inside of a cupping glass, make an incision in the patient's body, and then put the cupping-glass over the incision. As the inside of the cupping-glass cooled, a partial vacuum formed, drawing out the blood.

Flamineo asked the two women, "Are you ready?"

Both replied, "We are ready."

"Whither shall I go now?" Flamineo said. "Oh, Lucian, shall I go to thy ridiculous Purgatory! Shall I find Alexander the Great cobbling shoes, Pompey tagging points, and Julius Caesar making hair-buttons, Hannibal selling blacking, and Caesar Augustus crying 'Garlic!' in the marketplace, Charlemagne selling lists by the dozen, and King Pepin crying 'apples' in a cart drawn with one horse!"

Lucian was an ancient satirist.

Points were like shoelaces. Pompey's job in Purgatory was to affix metal tags to the ends of the laces, which were used to lace up clothing.

Hair-buttons were made with hair. This was the job of Julius Caesar, who was bald, in Purgatory.

Hannibal was swarthy because he was from Carthage, which was settled by Phoenicians. Blacking is black shoe polish.

"Lists" are strips of cloth.

A pippin is a variety of apple.

Flamineo then said, "Whether I decompose to fire, earth, water, air, or all the elements by tiny degrees, I don't know, nor greatly care."

He gave them the pistols and said, "Shoot! Shoot! Of all deaths, the violent death is best; for from ourselves it steals ourselves so fast that the pain, before it can be apprehended, is quite past."

In violent deaths, people often die quickly. Natural deaths often take a long, painful time.

Vittoria and Zanche shot at him, ran to him, and treaded on him.

Vittoria said viciously, "What! Have you dropped?"

Flamineo said, "I am mixed with earth already. As you are noble, perform your vows, and bravely follow me."

They had vowed to die, too.

"Follow you where?" Vittoria asked. "To hell?"

"To most assured damnation?" Zanche asked.

"Oh, thou most cursed devil!" Vittoria said.

Zanche began, "Thou are caught —"

Vittoria finished, "— in thine own engine. I tread out the fire that would have been my destruction."

"Will you be perjured?" Flamineo said. "What a religious oath was Styx, which the gods never dared to swear by and violate!"

Swearing by the River Styx was an inviolable oath: The gods *had* to do what they had sworn to do.

Flamineo continued, "Oh, that we had such an oath to minister, and to be so well kept in our courts of justice!"

Vittoria said, "Think whither thou are going."

Zanche said, "And remember what villainies thou have acted."

Vittoria said, "This thy death shall make me similar to a blazing ominous star — look up and tremble."

Flamineo said, "Oh, I am caught with a spring — a snare!"

Vittoria said, "You see the fox comes many times short home; it is here proved true."

A fox whose tail is caught in a trap can lose its tail, according to one of Aesop's fables.

Flamineo said, "Killed by a couple of hounds!"

Female hounds are bitches.

Vittoria said, "There is no fitter offing for the infernal Furies than one in whom they reigned while he was living."

Flamineo said, "Oh, the way's dark and horrid! I cannot see. Shall I have no company?"

"Oh, yes," Vittoria said, "thy sins run before thee to fetch fire from hell, to light for thee the way thither."

Flamineo said, "Oh, I smell soot, most stinking soot! The chimney's on fire; my liver's parboiled, like Scotch holy-bread."

Usually, holy-bread is bread used in the Eucharist, but Scotch holy-bread is a boiled sheep's liver.

Flamineo continued, "There's a plumber laying pipes in my guts — it scalds. Will thou outlive me?"

Zanche said, "Yes, and I will drive a stake through thy body; for we'll say that thou did this violence upon thyself."

When someone committed suicide, a stake was driven through their heart and they were buried at a crossroad.

Flamineo said, "Oh, cunning devils! Now I have tested your love, and doubled all your reaches: I am not wounded."

"Doubled all your reaches" meant "outstripped all your plots."

When pursued by a predator, rabbits double: They make evasive turns that make them hard to catch.

Flamineo, who was unhurt, stood up and said, "The pistols held no bullets; it was a plot to test your natural affection for me; and I live to punish your ingratitude.

"I knew that at one time or another you would find a way to give me a strong potion of poison.

"Oh, men who lie upon your deathbeds and are haunted with howling wives! Never trust them; they'll re-marry before the worm pierces your shroud, before the spider makes a thin curtain for your epitaphs.

"How cunning you were to discharge your pistols! Do you practice at the Artillery Yard?

"Trust a woman? Never, never: Brachiano is my precedent."

Brachiano was responsible for the murder of a woman: Isabella, his wife.

Flamineo continued, "We lay our souls to pawn to the devil for a little pleasure, and a woman makes the bill of sale.

"That a man should ever marry! For one Hypermnestra who saved her lord and husband, forty-nine of her sisters cut their husbands' throats all in one night."

In mythology, a man named Danaus was suspicious of Aegyptus and his fifty sons, who wanted to marry Danaus' fifty daughters, so he fled with his daughters, but Aegyptus and his fifty sons pursued them. To avoid a battle, Danaus told his fifty daughters to marry the fifty sons of Aegyptus, but although he allowed the marriages, he also ordered his fifty daughters to kill the fifty sons of Aegyptus. All of his daughters except Hypermnestra, who had married Lynceus, obeyed. Hypermnestra spared Lynceus because he treated her with respect and did not force her to have sex with him their first night together.

Flamineo continued, "There was a shoal of 'virtuous' horse leeches — blood-suckers!"

He drew his sword and his dagger and said, "Here are two other instruments."

Lodovico and Gasparo, still disguised as Capuchin monks, entered the room. Pedro and Carlo followed them.

"Help! Help!" Vittoria shouted.

"What noise is that?" Flamineo said.

Lodovico and Gasparo disarmed him.

"Ha!" Flamineo said. "False keys in the court!"

He had locked the door, but these men had been able to gain entry.

"We have brought you a masque," Lodovico said.

Many plays of the period had masques in which disguised revelers entered a party and invited those already there to dance.

Flamineo replied, "A matachin, it seems by your drawn swords."

A matachin is a sword-dance.

He added, "Churchmen turned revelers!"

Gasparo cried, "Isabella! Isabella!"

She was why they were there; they wanted to revenge her death.

Lodovico and Gasparo took off their disguises.

Lodovico asked, "Do you know us now?"

Flamineo said, "Lodovico! And Gasparo!"

"Yes," Lodovico said, "and that Moor the late Duke of Brachiano gave pension to was the great Duke of Florence."

"Oh, we are lost!" Vittoria said.

Flamineo said, "You shall not take justice forth from my hands. Oh, let me kill her!"

He wanted to be the one to kill his sister.

He said, "I'll cut my safety through your coats of steel."

He tried, but failed.

Flamineo then said, "Fate's a spaniel: We cannot beat it from us."

Cocker spaniels were reputed to stay faithful to their masters, even if their masters beat them.

Flamineo then asked, "What remains to be done now? Let all who do ill, take this precedent. Man may his fate foresee, but not prevent.

"And of all axioms this shall win the prize:

"It is better to be fortunate than wise."

Gasparo said, "Bind him to the pillar."

They did.

"Oh, your gentle pity!" Vittoria said. "I have seen a blackbird that would sooner fly to a man's bosom than to await the grip of the fierce sparrow-hawk."

Vittoria was like the blackbird: She would prefer to be in the clutches of Lodovico, Gasparo, Pedro, and Carlo than in the clutches of her brother.

"Your hope deceives you," Gasparo said.

Vittoria said, "If the Duke of Florence should be here in the court, I wish that he would kill me!"

"Fool!" Gasparo said. "Princes give rewards with their own hands, but death or punishment by the hands of other people."

Princes hire assassins rather than do the dirty work themselves.

Lodovico said to Flamineo, "Sirrah, you once did strike me; I'll strike you to the center."

By center, he meant both Flamineo's heart and the center of the earth.

In Dante's *Inferno*, hell is underground, and Lucifer is punished at the exact center of the earth.

Flamineo said, "Thou shall do it like a hangman, a base hangman, not like a noble fellow, for thou see I cannot strike again."

He was restrained and could not defend himself.

Lodovico asked, "Do thou laugh?"

Flamineo replied, "Would thou have me die, as I was born, in whining?"

"Recommend yourself to heaven," Gasparo said.

"No," Flamineo said. "I will carry my own commendations thither."

Lodovico said, "Oh, I could kill you forty times a day for four years, and it would still be too little!"

Killing Flamineo 58,440 times would be too few for Lodovico.

Lodovico continued, "Nothing grieves me except that you are too few to feed the famine of our vengeance."

He then asked Flamineo, "What do thou think about?"

Flamineo replied, "Nothing, of nothing: I think nothing of nothing.

"Put aside thy idle questions. I am in the way to study a long silence: To prate would be idle. I remember nothing. There's nothing of so infinite vexation as a man's own thoughts."

Lodovico said to Vittoria, "Oh, thou glorious strumpet! If I could divide thy breath from this pure air when thy soul leaves thy body, I would suck it up, and exhale it upon some dunghill."

Vittoria said, "You! My death's-man! I think thou do not look horrid enough. Thou have too good a face to be a hangman. If thou are an executioner, do thy office in the right form: Fall down upon thy knees, and ask forgiveness."

It was customary for executioners to ask the people whom they were going to execute to forgive them.

Lodovico replied, "Oh, thou have been a most prodigious comet!"

Comets were ill omens.

He said, "But I'll cut off your train."

He ordered, "Kill the Moor first."

The tails of comets were called trains. Members of the upper class had trains of attendants. Zanche was one of Vittoria's attendants.

Vittoria said, "You shall not kill her first; behold my breast. I will be waited on in death; my servant shall never go before me."

"Are you so brave?" Gasparo asked.

Vittoria replied, "Yes, I shall welcome death, as princes do some great ambassadors. I'll meet thy weapon halfway."

She would run upon his sword.

"Thou do tremble," Lodovico said "I think that fear should dissolve thee into air."

Vittoria replied, "Oh, thou are deceived! I am too true a woman! Conceit — mere imagination — can never kill me.

"I'll tell thee what — I will not in my death shed one base tear. If I should look pale, it will be for lack of blood; it will not be because of fear."

Carlo said to Zanche, "Thou are my task, black fury."

He would be the one to kill her.

Zanche said defiantly, "I have blood as red as either of theirs. Will thou drink some? It is good for the falling-sickness."

The falling-sickness is epilepsy, but she would fall after being run through with Carlo's sword.

She continued, "I am proud that death cannot alter my complexion, for I shall never look pale."

Her black skin would not be pale as she faced death.

Lodovico said, "Strike, strike, with a joint motion."

They stabbed Flamineo, Vittoria, and Zanche.

Zanche died immediately.

Vittoria said defiantly, "It was a 'manly' blow. The next blow thou give, murder some sucking infant, and then thou will be famous."

Flamineo knew that he was dying, but he remained defiant.

He said carelessly, "Oh, what blade is it thou used to stab me? A Toledo, or an English fox? I always thought a cutler should distinguish the cause of my death, rather than a doctor."

Toledo and English fox were different kinds of swords.

Many good swords were made in Toledo, Spain.

A cutler dealt in swords and knives.

Flamineo said, "Search my wound deeper; tent it with the steel that made it."

To search a wound means to probe it. A tent is a piece of absorbent material used to search and clean a wound.

Vittoria said, "Oh, my greatest sin lay in my blood! Now my blood pays for it."

The first use of "blood" meant passion. She could have been referring to sexual passion, or she could have been referring to a capacity for feeling strong emotion, including anger.

Flamineo said to her, "Thou are a noble sister! I love thee now. If a woman breeds a man, she ought to teach him manhood. Fare thee well."

He believed that she was dying bravely.

He continued, "Know that many glorious women who are famed for the masculine virtue of courage have been vicious, only a happier silence did befall them: Their viciousness was kept secret. A woman has no faults, if she has the skill to hide them."

Vittoria said, "My soul, like a ship in a black storm, is driven I don't know whither."

People, when they die, do not know their destination.

Flamineo said, "Then cast anchor. Prosperity bewitches men, because it appears clear. But seas do laugh, show white, when rocks are near.

"We cease to grieve, we cease to be fortune's slaves, and indeed we cease to die by dying."

He said to Zanche, "Are thou gone?"

She had died.

He then said to Vittoria, "And thou so near the bottom — so near death?

"It is a false report that says that women vie with the nine Muses for nine tough durable lives!"

It is a false report. Cats, not women, are said to have nine lives. The Muses are immortal.

A proverb stated, "A cat has nine lives, and a woman has nine cats' lives."

Flamineo continued, "I do not look at who went before, nor who shall follow me. No, at myself I will begin the end. While we look up to heaven, we confound knowledge with Knowledge."

Earthly knowledge is "knowledge"; heavenly wisdom is "Knowledge."

He said, "Oh, I am in a mist!"

This was a sign of swiftly approaching death.

Vittoria said, "Oh, happy are they who never saw the court, and never knew great men except by report!"

She died.

Flamineo said, "I recover like a spent candle, for a flash, and then instantly go out.

"Let all who belong to great men remember the old wives' tradition, to be like the lions in the Tower of London on Candlemas-day — February 2 — to mourn if the sun shine, for fear of the pitiful remainder of winter to come."

If the sun shone on that day, supposedly weeks of winter weather would follow.

Metaphorically, enjoying happiness out of season leads to much unhappiness later.

Flamineo continued, "It is well yet there's some goodness in my death. My life was a black charnel house where bones are stored."

He was dying bravely.

His voice giving out, he added, "I have caught an everlasting cold; I have lost my voice most irrecoverably.

"Farewell, glorious — boastful — villains.

"This busy activity of life appears most vain — empty and boastful — since rest breeds rest, where all seek pain by pain."

In a society where everyone works hard to protect themselves and their property and acquire more only to suffer pain and the need to work ever harder to be safe, rest leads to everlasting rest. Let down your guard, and you die.

Flamineo said his last words:

"Let no harsh flattering bells resound my knell;

"Strike, thunder, and strike loud, to my farewell!"

He died as young Giovanni, the six ambassadors, and some attendants arrived outside the room.

The English Ambassador shouted, "This way! This way! Break open the doors! This way!"

Lodovico said, "Ha! Are we betrayed? Why, then let's resolutely all die together, and having finished this most noble deed, defy the worst of fate, nor fear to bleed."

Young Giovanni, the six ambassadors, and some attendants broke open the door and entered the room.

The English Ambassador said, "Keep back the prince! Protect Giovanni! Shoot! Shoot!"

They shot Lodovico.

"Oh, I am wounded!" Lodovico said. "I fear I shall be captured."

"You bloody villains," young Giovanni said, "by what authority have you committed this massacre?"

"By thine," Lodovico said.

"Mine!" young Giovanni said.

Lodovico said, "Yes. The Duke of Florence, thy uncle, who is a part of thee, enjoined us to do it. Thou know who I am, I am sure. I am Count Lodovico, and thy most noble uncle — in disguise — was last night in thy court."

"Ha!" young Giovanni said.

Lodovico said, "Yes, he was that Moor thy father chose to be his pensioner. Your father gave him a pension."

Young Giovanni said, "He turned murderer!"

He then ordered, "Take them away to prison, and to torture. All who have hands in this shall taste our justice, as I have hope to go to heaven."

Lodovico said, "I glory yet that I can call this act my own. For my part, the rack, the gallows, and the torturing wheel shall be but sound sleeps to me.

"Here's my rest. I painted this night-piece, and it was my best."

The night-piece — a painting depicting a scene at night — was the massacre.

Giovanni ordered, "Remove these bodies."

He then said, "See, my honored lords, what use you ought to make of their punishment.

"Let guilty men remember, their black deeds

"Do lean on crutches made of slender reeds."

NON-EPILOGUE

Instead of an epilogue, only this of Martial supplies me:

Haec fuerint nobis præmia, si placui.

Translated from Martial *Epigrammata*, II, xci, 8, the Latin means this:

"These things shall be my reward, if I have pleased you."

In other words: Your applause and approval shall be my rewards.

APPENDIX A: NOTES

— 1.2 —

Lycurgus wondered much, men would provide
*   Good stallions for their mares, and yet would suffer [allow]*
*   Their fair wives to be barren. (1.2.340-342)*

Source of Above: John Webster, *The White Devil*. Ed. Christina Luckyj. 2nd Edition. The New Mermaids. London and New York: A & C Black and W W Norton, 1978.

John Webster (or Flamineo) misunderstood, at least partly, Lycurgus, who was concerned about eugenics. No doubt, however, he was also concerned about barrenness.

The passage below is from *Primitive Love and Love-stories*, by Henry Theophilus Finck. In the section GREEK LOVE-STORIES AND POEMS appears this sub-section: SPARTAN OPPORTUNITIES FOR LOVE:

Had Plato lived a few centuries earlier he might have visited at least one Greek state where his barbarous ideal of the sexual relations was to a considerable extent realized. The Spartan law-maker Lycurgus shared his views regarding marriage, and had the advantage of being able to enforce them. He, too, believed that human beings should be bred like cattle. He laughed, so Plutarch tells us in his biographic sketch, at those who, while exercising care in raising dogs and horses, allowed unworthy husbands to have offspring. This, in itself, was a praiseworthy thought; but the method adopted by Lycurgus to overcome that objection was subversive of all morality and affection. He considered it advisable that among worthy men there should be a community of wives and children, for which purpose he tried to suppress jealousy, ridiculing those who insisted on a conjugal monopoly and who even engaged in fights on account of it. Elderly men were urged to share their wives with younger men and adopt the children as their own; and if a man considered another's wife particularly prolific or virtuous he was not to hesitate to ask for her.

Source of Above: Henry Theophilus Finck, *Primitive Love and Love-stories*. New York: Charles Scribner's Sons, 1899. Page 776.

<https://tinyurl.com/vxf2b9z>

***

The passage below comes from Plutarch's *Life of Lycurgus*:

6 After giving marriage such traits of reserve and decorum, he none the less freed men from the empty and womanish passion of jealous possession, by making it honourable for them, while keeping the marriage relation free from all wanton irregularities, to share with other worthy men in the begetting of children, laughing to scorn those who regard such common privileges as intolerable, and resort to murder and war rather than grant them. 7 For example, an elderly man with a young wife, if he looked with favour and esteem on some fair and noble young man, might introduce him to her, and adopt her offspring by such a noble father as his p253 own. And again, a worthy man who admired some woman for the fine children that she bore her husband and the modesty of her behaviour as a wife, might enjoy her favours, if her husband would consent, thus planting, as it were, in a soil of bountiful fruitage, and begetting for himself noble sons, who would have the blood of noble men in their veins. 8 For in the first place, Lycurgus did not regard sons as the peculiar property of their fathers, but rather as the common property of the state, and therefore would not have his citizens spring from random parentage, but from the best there was. In the second place, he saw much folly and vanity in what other peoples enacted for the regulation of these matters; in the breeding of dogs and horses they insist on having the best sires which money or favour can secure, but they keep their wives under lock and key, demanding that they have children by none but themselves, even though they be foolish, or infirm, or diseased; 9 as though children of bad stock did not show their badness to those first who possessed and reared them, and children of good stock, contrariwise, their goodness. The freedom which thus prevailed at that time in marriage relations was aimed at physical and political well-being, and was far removed from the licentiousness which was afterwards attributed to their women, so much so that adultery was wholly unknown among them. 10 And a saying is reported of one Geradas, 15, a Spartan of very ancient type, who, on being asked by a stranger what the punishment for adulterers was among them, answered: "Stranger, p255 there is no adulterer among us." "Suppose, then," replied the stranger, "there should be one." "A bull," said Geradas, "would be his forfeit, a bull so large that it could stretch over Mount Taÿgetus and drink from the river Eurotas." Then the stranger was astonished and said: "But how could there be a bull so large?" To which

*Geradas replied, with a smile: "But how could there be an adulterer in Sparta?"
Such, then, are the accounts we find of their marriages.*

Source of Above: Plutarch. *Life of Lycurgus. The Parallel Lives* by Plutarch published in Vol. I of the Loeb Classical Library edition, 1914. The text is in the public domain.

<http://penelope.uchicago.edu/Thayer/E/Roman/Texts/Plutarch/Lives/home.html>

<https://tinyurl.com/5ufwsd>

— 1.2 —

[...] *under that yew,*

As I sat sadly leaning on a grave,

Checkered with cross-sticks, [...] (1.2.233-235)

Source of Above: John Webster, *The White Devil*. Ed. Christina Luckyj. 2nd Edition. The New Mermaids. London and New York: A & C Black and W W Norton, 1978.

Ben Jonson's *The Masque of Queens* has a reference to "Sticks are a-cross" and a Note explaining what that means:

The Reference:

The Sticks are a-cross, there can be no loss,

The Sage is rotten, the Sulphur is gotten

Up to the Sky, that was i'th' ground.

Follow it then, with our Rattles, round;

The Note:

This throwing of ashes, and sand, with the flint-stone, cross sticks, and burying of Sage, &c. are all us'd (and believ'd by them) to the raising of storm, and tempest.

Source of Above: Ben Jonson, *The Masque of Queens*. Luminarium. Accessed 10 December 2019

<https://www.hollowaypages.com/jonson1692fame.htm>

The *Oxford English Dictionary* defines "chequered" in this way:

To put or place alternately. Obsolete. nonce-use *(with word-play).*

a1661 T. Fuller Worthies (1662) Surrey 81 In the reign of King Henry the Third, when Chancellors were chequered in and out, three times he discharged that office.

But perhaps it is not a nonce-use.

— 1.2 —

The subtle foldings of a winter's snake, (1.2.350)

Source of Above: John Webster, *The White Devil*. Ed. Christina Luckyj. 2nd Edition. The New Mermaids. London and New York: A & C Black and W W Norton, 1978.

Below is some information from Snakeprotection.com:

Snakes less active in winter, but don't hibernate

Snakes do not actually hibernate, rather they become less active during cold weather. It is called "brumation." Brumation is an extreme slowing down of their metabolism. Snakes are awake, but just very lethargic so you don't see them moving around. In the fall, snakes move back to the previous year's den. If a sudden cold snap catches them before they get there, they may die if not fortunate enough to find a suitable secondary den. They usually do not stay long at the den entrance, but hurry in for the long winter sleep. A number of species may share the same den. For example, black rat snakes, timber rattlesnakes and copperheads commonly den together. Sometimes there will be as many as 100 snakes in one cave. A group site is called a hibernaculum.

Source of Above: "Snakes less active in winter, but don't hibernate." Snakeprotection.com. 29 October 2015 <https://tinyurl.com/s5d9sob>.

— **2.2** —

Fellows indeed that live only by stealth,

Since they do merely lie about stol'n goods, (2.2.17-18)

Source of Above: John Webster, *The White Devil*. Ed. Christina Luckyj. 2nd Edition. The New Mermaids. London and New York: A & C Black and W W Norton, 1978.

Even today, astrologers claim to be able to locate stolen goods and to identify the thief. See these Web pages:

1) Astrologer Dheeraj Pareek, "Article: How to use astrology to recover stolen items?" GoAstrologer. Accessed 15 December 2019

<https://tinyurl.com/u7m4qp4>.

"So,this time you want to know How to use astrology to recover stolen items ? That's pretty interesting question.We can find lost and stolen items through astrology.You can find your stolen objects through prabhas jyotish.Nakshatra Astrology,numerology etc. We will clear these top three methods to find a stolen object."

2) "How To Know About The Lost and Stolen Item." TRUTHSTAR. December 2019

<https://tinyurl.com/vg2lmbf>.

"Lost and Stolen Item – If the seventh lord of Prashan kundali is Jupiter, in that case a respectable person like – Guru, Brahmin, Teacher or Officer can be a thief who steals the item with the help of others."

— 3.2 —

You see my lords what goodly fruit she seems,
*   Yet like those apples travelers report*
*   To grow where Sodom and Gomorrah stood:*
*   I will touch her and you straight shall see*
*   She'll fall to soot and ashes.* (3.2.63-67)

Source of Above: John Webster, *The White Devil*. Ed. Christina Luckyj. 2nd Edition. The New Mermaids. London and New York: A & C Black and W W Norton, 1978.

Sir John Mandeville wrote this in his travel book:

By the ides of this sea grow trees that bear apples fine of colour and delightful to look at; but when they are broken or cut, only ashes and dust and cinders are found inside, as a token of the vengeance that God took on those five cities [including Sodom and Gomorrah] and the countryside round about, burning them with the fires of Hell.

Source: Sir John Mandeville, *The Travels of Sir John Mandeville*. C. W. R. D. Moseley, ed. Penguin, 2005.

<https://tinyurl.com/rk5usrd>.

Look you, six grey rats that have lost their tails
    Crawl up the pillow. Send for a rat-catcher. (5.3.124-125)
    Source of Above: John Webster, *The White Devil*. Ed. Christina Luckyj. 2nd Edition. The New Mermaids. London and New York: A & C Black and W W Norton, 1978.
    The note below on a line from *Macbeth* comes from the following book:
    The Works of William Shakepeare: Volume V. Edited by Henry Irving and Frank A Marshall. With Notes and Introductions To Each Play By F. A. Marshall and Other Shakespearian Scholars. London: Blackie & Son, 49 & 50 Old Bailey, [?]C; Glasgow, Edinburgh, And Dublin. 1889.
    <https://tinyurl.com/t35vof3>
    And, like a rat without a tail. — *Steevens says "that though a witch could assume the form of any animal she pleased, the tail would still be wanting" (Var. Ed. vol. xL p. 32). He then goes on to state "the reasons given by some of the old writers.' I cannot find anything on this subject in Reginald Scot's Discoverie of Witchcraft, though he has a great deal to say about the transformation of witches (book v.). In Thiselton Dyer's Folk Lore of Shakespeare (p. 80) the author says: "In German legends and traditions, we find frequent notice of witches, assuming the form of a cat, and displaying their fiendish character in certain diabolical acts. It was, however, the absence of the tail that only too often was the cause of the witch being detected in her disguised form." That horrible creature of superstition, the were-wolf, or human being changed into a wolf, was distinguished by having no tail. The most usual form for a witch to take was that of a cat or wolf, or mouse, or goat sometimes of a hare, not very often of a rat; though rats have always been looked upon as uncanny creatures and connected, more or less, with the devil. The only historical demon-rat that I remember is that one in Dickens's amusing article Nurses' Stories, in The Uncommercial Traveller. How that diabolical animal persecuted the unfortunate Chips will be remembered by readers of that amusing work. Capell suggests another explanation of* without a tail, *that as tails are the rudders of such animals as the water-rat, the witch means she could do without a rudder as well as sail in a sieve.* — *F. A. M.*

Study my prayers! He threatens me divinely! I am
   falling to pieces already — I care not, though,
   like Anacharsis, I were pounded to death in a mortar. And
   yet that death were fitter for usurers' gold and them-
   selves to be beaten together to make a most cordial
   cullis for the devil. (5.4.23-28)

Source of Above: John Webster, *The White Devil*. Ed. Christina Luckyj. 2nd Edition. The New Mermaids. London and New York: A & C Black and W W Norton, 1978.

The death of Anaxarchus is told in Diogenes Laërtius' *Lives of Eminent Philosophers*, ix. 58:

Ch. 10. ANAXARCHUS

[58] Anaxarchus, a native of Abdera, studied under Diogenes of Smyrna, and the latter under Metrodorus of Chios, who used to declare that he knew nothing, not even the fact that he knew nothing ; while Metrodorus was a pupil of Nessas of Chios, though some say that he was taught by Democritus. Now Anaxarchus accompanied Alexander and flourished in the 110th Olympiad. He made an enemy of Nicocreon, tyrant of Cyprus. Once at a banquet, when asked by Alexander how he liked the feast, he is said to have answered, "Everything, O king, is magnificent ; there is only one thing lacking, that the head of some satrap should be served up at table." This was a hit at Nicocreon, [59] who never forgot it, and when after the king's death Anaxarchus was forced against his will to land in Cyprus, he seized him and, putting him in a mortar, ordered him to be pounded to death with iron pestles. But he, making light of the punishment, made that well-known speech, "Pound, pound the pouch containing Anaxarchus ; ye pound not Anaxarchus." And when Nicocreon commanded his tongue to be cut out, they say he bit it off and spat it at him. This is what I have written upon him :

"Pound, Nicocreon, as hard as you like : it is but a pouch. Pound on ; Anaxarchus's self long since is housed with Zeus. And after she has drawn you upon her carding-combs a little while, Persephone will utter words like these: 'Out upon thee, villainous miller !'"

[60] For his fortitude and contentment in life he was called the Happy Man. He had, too, the capacity of bringing anyone to reason in the easiest possible way. At all events he succeeded in diverting Alexander when he had begun to think himself a god; for, seeing blood running from a wound he had sustained, he pointed to him with his finger and said,

"See, there is blood and not Ichor which courses in the veins of the blessed gods."

Plutarch reports this as spoken by Alexander to his friends. Moreover, on another occasion, when Anaxarchus was drinking Alexander's health, he held up his goblet and said :

"One of the gods shall fall by the stroke of mortal man."

Source: of Above:

Diogenes Laërtius, *Lives of Eminent Philosophers.*

R.D. Hicks, Translator. Cambridge. Harvard University Press. 1972 (First published 1925). Book 9. Chapter 10. Sections 58-60.

<https://tinyurl.com/uug6sgg>

— 5.4 —

"Call for the robin-red-breast, and the wren, (5.4.92)

Source of Above: John Webster, *The White Devil*. Ed. Christina Luckyj. 2nd Edition. The New Mermaids. London and New York: A & C Black and W W Norton, 1978.

An entry in the Oxford University Press Blog states this:

For some reason, in oral tradition, the robin is often connected with the wren. In Surrey (a county bordering London), and not only there, people used to say: "The robin and the wren are God's cock and hen" (as though the wren were the female of the robin, but then the wren is indeed Jenny).

Source of Above: Anatoly Liberman, "The robin and the wren." Oxford University Press Blog. 16 January 2019

<https://blog.oup.com/2019/01/robin-and-the-wren/>

<https://tinyurl.com/tfagke6>

— 5.6 —

You see the fox comes many times short home;
'Tis here proved true. (5.6.134-135)

Source of Above: John Webster, *The White Devil*. Ed. Christina Luckyj. 2nd Edition. The New Mermaids. London and New York: A & C Black and W W Norton, 1978.

Aesop: "The Fox Who Had Lost Its Tale [Tail]."

A FOX, caught in a trap, escaped with the loss of his brush [bushy tail]. Henceforth, feeling his life a burden from the shame and ridicule to which he was exposed, he schemed to bring all the other Foxes into a like condition with himself.

He publicly advised them to cut off their tails, saying that they would not only look much better without them, but that they would get rid of the weight of the brush. One of them said: If you had not yourself lost your tail, my friend, you would not thus counsel us.

Source of Above: Aesop. Translator Unknown. "The Fox Who Had Lost Its Tale." Litscapecom. Accessed 4 January 2020

<https://www.litscape.com/author/Aesop/ The_Fox_Who_Had_Lost_His_Tail.html>.

— 5.6 —

False report
  Which says that women vie with the nine Muses
  For nine tough durable lives! (5.6.252-254)
Source of Above: John Webster, *The White Devil*. Ed. Christina Luckyj. 2nd Edition. The New Mermaids. London and New York: A & C Black and W W Norton, 1978.

The below is part of a note for Ben Jonson's *Every Man in His Humour*:

It is recorded also in Hazlitt's English Proverbs and Proverbial Phrases, *p. 5: "A cat has nine lives, and a woman has nine cats' lives." The following are typical examples from literature: Middleton* Blurt, Master Constable *I. 287: "They have nine lives apiece (like a woman), and they will make it up ten lives, if they and I fall a-scratching" [...].*

Source of Above: Ben Jonson, *Every Man in His Humour*, Volume 52. Henry Holland Carter, ed. New Haven: Yale University Press. London: Humphrey Milford. Oxford University Press. 1921. P. 344.
  <https://tinyurl.com/w2t9s46>.

— Entire Play —

Who is the white devil?

A proverb stated, "The white devil is worse than the black."

A white devil is an evil person who pretends to be a good person.

Possibly, a white devil is a good person whom everyone believes to be evil.

Certainly, this play has many hypocrites.

Some people probably think that Vittoria is the white devil, but has she really committed evil? Many people in the play think that she has committed adultery, but has she? She was tempted, but she did not commit adultery in 1.2 because of being interrupted. Her trial was biased and did not produce evidence of adultery. If she is the white devil, and if she is innocent of major wrongdoing, perhaps the play ought to be titled *The "White" Devil*.

But she may very well be a white devil if the dream she recounts in 1.2 really is a coded message to Brachiano to kill her husband and his wife.

Many characters in the play are evil, but even they can have redeeming features. Flamineo dies bravely, continuing his defiance to the end.

Perhaps a white devil is an evil person with some redeeming features.

Perhaps John Webster meant that all of us are hypocrites in one way or another. After all, all of us have sinned.

Young Giovanni may not have sinned, but he is young. He does order some people to be tortured, but his society would probably think that the torture is justified.

Maybe the play should have been titled *The White Devils*.

APPENDIX B: ABOUT THE AUTHOR

It was a dark and stormy night. Suddenly a cry rang out, and on a hot summer night in 1954, Josephine, wife of Carl Bruce, gave birth to a boy — me. Unfortunately, this young married couple allowed Reuben Saturday, Josephine's brother, to name their first-born. Reuben, aka "The Joker," decided that Bruce was a nice name, so he decided to name me Bruce Bruce. I have gone by my middle name — David — ever since.

Being named Bruce David Bruce hasn't been all bad. Bank tellers remember me very quickly, so I don't often have to show an ID. It can be fun in charades, also. When I was a counselor as a teenager at Camp Echoing Hills in Warsaw, Ohio, a fellow counselor gave the signs for "sounds like" and "two words," then she pointed to a bruise on her leg twice. Bruise Bruise? Oh yeah, Bruce Bruce is the answer!

Uncle Reuben, by the way, gave me a haircut when I was in kindergarten. He cut my hair short and shaved a small bald spot on the back of my head. My mother wouldn't let me go to school until the bald spot grew out again.

Of all my brothers and sisters (six in all), I am the only transplant to Athens, Ohio. I was born in Newark, Ohio, and have lived all around Southeastern Ohio. However, I moved to Athens to go to Ohio University and have never left.

At Ohio U, I never could make up my mind whether to major in English or Philosophy, so I got a Bachelor's with a double major in both areas in 1980, then I added a Master's in English in 1984 and a Master's in Philosophy in 1985. Currently, I am a retired English instructor at Ohio U.

If all goes well, I will publish one or two books a year for the rest of my life. (On the other hand, a good way to make God laugh is to tell Her your plans.)

By the way, my sister Brenda Kennedy writes romances such as *A New Beginning* and *Shattered Dreams*.

APPENDIX C: SOME BOOKS BY DAVID BRUCE

Retellings of a Classic Work of Literature

Arden of Faversham: *A Retelling*

Ben Jonson's The Alchemist: *A Retelling*

Ben Jonson's The Arraignment, or Poetaster: *A Retelling*

Ben Jonson's Bartholomew Fair: *A Retelling*

Ben Jonson's The Case is Altered: *A Retelling*

Ben Jonson's Catiline's Conspiracy: *A Retelling*

Ben Jonson's The Devil is an Ass: *A Retelling*

Ben Jonson's Epicene: *A Retelling*

Ben Jonson's Every Man in His Humor: *A Retelling*

Ben Jonson's Every Man Out of His Humor: *A Retelling*

Ben Jonson's The Fountain of Self-Love, or Cynthia's Revels: *A Retelling*

Ben Jonson's The Magnetic Lady, or Humors Reconciled: *A Retelling*

Ben Jonson's The New Inn, or The Light Heart: *A Retelling*

Ben Jonson's Sejanus' Fall: *A Retelling*

Ben Jonson's The Staple of News: *A Retelling*

Ben Jonson's A Tale of a Tub: *A Retelling*

Ben Jonson's Volpone, or the Fox: *A Retelling*

Christopher Marlowe's Complete Plays: Retellings

Christopher Marlowe's Dido, Queen of Carthage: *A Retelling*

Christopher Marlowe's Doctor Faustus: *Retellings of the 1604 A-Text and of the 1616 B-Text*

Christopher Marlowe's Edward II: *A Retelling*

Christopher Marlowe's The Massacre at Paris: *A Retelling*

Christopher Marlowe's The Rich Jew of Malta: *A Retelling*

Christopher Marlowe's Tamburlaine, Parts 1 and 2: *Retellings*

Dante's Divine Comedy: *A Retelling in Prose*

Dante's Inferno: *A Retelling in Prose*

Dante's Purgatory: *A Retelling in Prose*

Dante's Paradise: *A Retelling in Prose*

The Famous Victories of Henry V: *A Retelling*

From the Iliad *to the* Odyssey: *A Retelling in Prose of Quintus of Smyrna's* Posthomerica

George Chapman, Ben Jonson, and John Marston's Eastward Ho! *A Retelling*

George Peele's The Arraignment of Paris: *A Retelling*

George Peele's The Battle of Alcazar: *A Retelling*

George Peele's David and Bathsheba, and the Tragedy of Absalom: *A Retelling*

George Peele's Edward I: *A Retelling*

George Peele's The Old Wives' Tale: *A Retelling*

George-a-Greene: *A Retelling*

The History of King Leir: *A Retelling*

Homer's Iliad: *A Retelling in Prose*

Homer's Odyssey: *A Retelling in Prose*

J.W. Gent.'s The Valiant Scot: *A Retelling*

Jason and the Argonauts: A Retelling in Prose of Apollonius of Rhodes' Argonautica

John Ford: Eight Plays Translated into Modern English

John Ford's The Broken Heart: *A Retelling*

John Ford's The Fancies, Chaste and Noble: *A Retelling*

John Ford's The Lady's Trial: *A Retelling*

John Ford's The Lover's Melancholy: *A Retelling*

John Ford's Love's Sacrifice: *A Retelling*

John Ford's Perkin Warbeck: *A Retelling*

John Ford's The Queen: *A Retelling*

John Ford's 'Tis Pity She's a Whore: *A Retelling*

John Lyly's Campaspe: *A Retelling*

John Lyly's Endymion, The Man in the Moon: *A Retelling*

John Lyly's Galatea: *A Retelling*

John Lyly's Love's Metamorphosis: *A Retelling*

John Lyly's Midas: *A Retelling*

John Lyly's Mother Bombie: *A Retelling*

John Lyly's Sappho and Phao: *A Retelling*

John Lyly's The Woman in the Moon: *A Retelling*

John Webster's The White Devil: *A Retelling*

King Edward III: *A Retelling*

Mankind: *A Medieval Morality Play* (A Retelling)

Margaret Cavendish's The Unnatural Tragedy: *A Retelling*

The Merry Devil of Edmonton: *A Retelling*

The Summoning of Everyman: *A Medieval Morality Play* (A Retelling)

Robert Greene's Friar Bacon and Friar Bungay: *A Retelling*

The Taming of a Shrew: *A Retelling*

Tarlton's Jests: A Retelling

Thomas Middleton's A Chaste Maid in Cheapside: *A Retelling*

Thomas Middleton's Women Beware Women: *A Retelling*

Thomas Middleton and Thomas Dekker's The Roaring Girl: *A Retelling*

Thomas Middleton and William Rowley's The Changeling: *A Retelling*

The Trojan War and Its Aftermath: Four Ancient Epic Poems

Virgil's Aeneid: *A Retelling in Prose*

William Shakespeare's 5 Late Romances: Retellings in Prose

William Shakespeare's 10 Histories: Retellings in Prose

William Shakespeare's 11 Tragedies: Retellings in Prose

William Shakespeare's 12 Comedies: Retellings in Prose

William Shakespeare's 38 Plays: Retellings in Prose
William Shakespeare's 1 Henry IV, aka Henry IV, Part 1: *A Retelling in Prose*
William Shakespeare's 2 Henry IV, aka Henry IV, Part 2: *A Retelling in Prose*
William Shakespeare's 1 Henry VI, aka Henry VI, Part 1: *A Retelling in Prose*
William Shakespeare's 2 Henry VI, aka Henry VI, Part 2: *A Retelling in Prose*
William Shakespeare's 3 Henry VI, aka Henry VI, Part 3: *A Retelling in Prose*
William Shakespeare's All's Well that Ends Well: *A Retelling in Prose*
William Shakespeare's Antony and Cleopatra: *A Retelling in Prose*
William Shakespeare's As You Like It: *A Retelling in Prose*
William Shakespeare's The Comedy of Errors: *A Retelling in Prose*
William Shakespeare's Coriolanus: *A Retelling in Prose*
William Shakespeare's Cymbeline: *A Retelling in Prose*
William Shakespeare's Hamlet: *A Retelling in Prose*
William Shakespeare's Henry V: *A Retelling in Prose*
William Shakespeare's Henry VIII: *A Retelling in Prose*
William Shakespeare's Julius Caesar: *A Retelling in Prose*
William Shakespeare's King John: *A Retelling in Prose*
William Shakespeare's King Lear: *A Retelling in Prose*
William Shakespeare's Love's Labor's Lost: *A Retelling in Prose*
William Shakespeare's Macbeth: *A Retelling in Prose*
William Shakespeare's Measure for Measure: *A Retelling in Prose*
William Shakespeare's The Merchant of Venice: *A Retelling in Prose*
William Shakespeare's The Merry Wives of Windsor: *A Retelling in Prose*
William Shakespeare's A Midsummer Night's Dream: *A Retelling in Prose*
William Shakespeare's Much Ado About Nothing: *A Retelling in Prose*
William Shakespeare's Othello: *A Retelling in Prose*
William Shakespeare's Pericles, Prince of Tyre: *A Retelling in Prose*
William Shakespeare's Richard II: *A Retelling in Prose*
William Shakespeare's Richard III: *A Retelling in Prose*
William Shakespeare's Romeo and Juliet: *A Retelling in Prose*
William Shakespeare's The Taming of the Shrew: *A Retelling in Prose*
William Shakespeare's The Tempest: *A Retelling in Prose*
William Shakespeare's Timon of Athens: *A Retelling in Prose*
William Shakespeare's Titus Andronicus: *A Retelling in Prose*
William Shakespeare's Troilus and Cressida: *A Retelling in Prose*
William Shakespeare's Twelfth Night: *A Retelling in Prose*
William Shakespeare's The Two Gentlemen of Verona: *A Retelling in Prose*
William Shakespeare's The Two Noble Kinsmen: *A Retelling in Prose*
William Shakespeare's The Winter's Tale: *A Retelling in Prose*